LP POTTER

Potter, Jay Hill.
Murder trail.

D1607850

ATCHISON LIBRARY
401 KANSAS
ATCHISON, KS 66002

SPECIAL MESSAGE TO READERS

This book is published under the auspices of
THE ULVERSCROFT FOUNDATION
(registered charity No. 264873 UK)

Established in 1972 to provide funds for
research, diagnosis and treatment of eye diseases.
Examples of contributions made are: —

A new Children's Assessment Unit at
Moorfield's Hospital, London.

•

Twin operating theatres at the
Western Ophthalmic Hospital, London.

•

A Chair of Ophthalmology at the
University of Leicester.

•

The establishment of a Royal Australian College
of Ophthalmologists "Fellowship".

You can help further the work of the Foundation
by making a donation or leaving a legacy. Every
contribution, no matter how small, is received
with gratitude. Please write for details to:

**THE ULVERSCROFT FOUNDATION,
The Green, Bradgate Road, Anstey,
Leicester LE7 7FU, England.
Telephone: (0116) 236 4325**

**In Australia write to:
THE ULVERSCROFT FOUNDATION,
c/o The Royal Australian College of
Ophthalmologists,
27, Commonwealth Street, Sydney,
N.S.W. 2010.**

MURDER TRAIL

Two professional killers have a list of names, the last one belonging to an ex-Texas Ranger shotgunned to death in a quiet town. The local sheriff hires troubleshooter and manhunter Cap'n Ed Gallion and the hunt is on for the murderers who have earlier eliminated three other Rangers. But why? Do the answers lie in the wilder past? Gallion and his friends ride a tortuous and bloody trail before they reach the terrible denouement.

JAY HILL POTTER

MURDER TRAIL

Complete and Unabridged

LINFORD
Leicester

First published in Great Britain in 1993 by
Robert Hale Limited
London

First Linford Edition
published 1996
by arrangement with
Robert Hale Limited
London

T 73544

The right of Jay Hill Potter to be identified as
the author of this work has been asserted by him
in accordance with the
Copyright, Designs and Patents Act, 1988

Copyright © 1993 by Jay Hill Potter
All rights reserved

British Library CIP Data

Potter, Jay Hill
    Murder trail.—Large print ed.—
Linford western library
1. English fiction—20th century
I. Title II. Series
823.9'14 [F]

ISBN 0–7089–7882–7

Published by
F. A. Thorpe (Publishing) Ltd.
Anstey, Leicestershire

Set by Words & Graphics Ltd.
Anstey, Leicestershire
Printed and bound in Great Britain by
T. J. Press (Padstow) Ltd., Padstow, Cornwall

LP WES POT
Potter, Jay Hill.
    Murder trail

1

A QUARTET of killings. The biggest job they had ever had. But could it be called one job, or was it four? Were they separate jobs or were they all part of the whole?

Pinker obviously didn't know. Didn't care either. He was enjoying himself mightily. Rimrock had never seen him so cock-a-hoop and happy.

Reckless, though, also. A cocky what-the-hell they-can't-touch-me attitude now that Rimrock didn't like at all.

The first one! It was actually two, though. Not good.

The man they wanted turned out to be a real home body. It was almost as if he were hiding from something.

He had a smallholding on the edge of the little town where he lived with his wife and a growing son who was at school when Rimrock and Pinker

1

ATCHISON LIBRARY
401 KANSAS
ATCHISON, KS 66002

called. It was a bright morning. Pinker, even though he was no Injun, had always said he didn't like working by night.

It was Rimrock's private opinion that Pinker actually enjoyed the greater danger of the day. To him a bright day was the time for killing. Then he could well see what he was about.

They caught the man while he was feeding his many noisy, healthy-looking chickens. A tall feller with an affable but wary manner, a gun tucked in the front of his belt as if he expected trouble at any time.

Pinker, charming as hell, spoke the man's name and the man answered to it. He had an almost empty feeding bowl in his right hand and the chickens bustled and clucked around his legs.

Rimrock figured from the position of the gun in the man's pants — the way the butt was pointing — that he was a right-handed man. Rimrock noticed things like that. He didn't stand a chance, though, that jasper, for Pinker

2

was pretty fast anyway.

Pinker drew his gun and shot the man in the head, the blood quickly blanketing the staring, incredulous face.

Neither of them had at first spotted the woman, though she could have been outside the door when Pinker fired the shot.

She screamed. It was an involuntary sound. Forced from her by shock and outrage. But then she did the sensible thing. She turned and moved back.

Pinker ran after her, holstering his gun as if he didn't need it now.

Rimrock went after Pinker. The woman reached her door, was reaching for the rifle leaning against the side of it when Pinker drew his knife from the back of his belt and threw it.

She was banged forward into the door, the knife sticking from her back like a strange growth. Just the butt. It had been a powerful throw and Pinker was good with that blade. It had gone in deeply.

The door was ajar. The woman went

through it, falling all the way.

Pinker rolled her over, retrieved his knife, wiped it on her skirt. She was obviously dead, her eyes staring as Pinker turned her over on to her back; then there was no blood at all.

Pinker made a tiny explosive sound. It could not be called a laugh. "Look at the way she's looking at me," he said. "She ain't as old as I expected. A fine piece of womanflesh."

He bent again after he had sheathed his weapon. He began to strip the woman.

Rimrock reached down and gripped Pinker's shoulder, squeezed it. "That shot easily could've been heard," he said. "We've got to get out of here. If you don't come right now I'm goin' without you."

Pinker turned his head and looked up at his partner, a strange hot look in his usually cold eyes which would twinkle so well when he was charming somebody. He pulled his hat over those eyes, shading them, as he straightened up, unspeaking.

Rimrock led the way out. Pinker followed him almost doglike. A lean soft-moving hound. They got their horses from the other side of the small corral, and they mounted up and rode away. They didn't see a soul except some cowboys and a few heads of beef. And that was miles on.

Rimrock thought of the woman, lying back there. Sort of sprawled indolently, carelessly. Younger than he had expected her to be. Her abundant brown hair haloed round her head, her full lips slightly apart, her eyes staring. The body that was good even in the work-clothes. The good body that was dead.

Rimrock's face began to itch. His bad face! The red face that had been like that ever since he was a youth. Not a natural sunburned face, but one that looked as if it had been *boiled* by sun, as if the sun had become molten and fallen down upon it, bathed it.

5

A redness that would not go away, and an itch that came and went.

Rimrock had often wondered whether if he settled down and lived a quiet life the itch would go away. Maybe if he lived to be old he could rest. But he could not rest now. He was as restless as his partner but in a sort of different way. He didn't know what was eating Pinker, knew nothing really *about* Pinker . . .

Then they were on to the second job. I'll handle this one, Rimrock thought, and I'll handle it better.

But the first job had gotten done anyway after all, hadn't it? Pinker had done it and he was away free. They were both away free.

The devil rode with Pinker and looked after him.

I ain't just the dust on Pinker's coat-tails though, Rimrock thought. I ain't afraid of Pinker or his devil. I'm my own man. When this four-part job is over that'll be the end of it and I'll go it alone again.

Four jobs in one though, and anything could happen. Would Pinker's devil continue to look out for Pinker? Hell, I'll stay with it anyway, Rimrock thought. With all that *dinero* I'd be a jackass if I didn't. They wouldn't get the other half of their pay till the job was all completed. And they had their reps in the business to keep up too, didn't they?

The way Pinker operated, Rimrock thought, the recklessness, the joyous killing, Pinker's string is sure to run out sooner or later. So, at the end, Rimrock concluded, I've gotta get rid of him like a prickly burr outa my ass.

2

THE second job was harder in that they had to get in and get their man. It was almost as if, like the first one, this one was sort of hiding, but in a different way and in a different sort of situation and place.

They knew the place. And they were known there, and that of course could be a drawback.

It was what could be called a wide-open town. It was in fact little more than an outlaw stronghold which had no law at all except for that made by the folks who lived there. There were some who were permanent. Ran good businesses; if of a somewhat nefarious nature.

Pinker and Rimrock entered by night. They took a room in what was grandly called a hotel but was nothing but a flea-ridden sort of bunkhouse that might have belonged to a particularly dirty ranch. There was no ranch anywhere around there though, for it was particularly barren country and the town was partially hidden in folds of low hills like outsize antheaps, suiting its denizens and visitors right down to the ground.

They passed themselves off as friends of the man they were after but said they didn't want to bother him so late at night, they'd call on him in the morning as a sort of surprise. It was easy to find out where he was at.

They got the information from a drunk in the next room after charming Pinker stroked his palm with silver as only Pinker could. The smiling killer whose eyes could turn to ice had a way with him that could have charmed the pantaloons off'n an old maid with cast-iron corsets — or so Rimrock said.

They both laughed. Rimrock had a sense of humour. He wondered if Pinker had. Or were his smiles, twinkles and chuckles all part of a man playing a part like an actor in a travelling fit-up group Rimrock had seen? And, come to think of it, the leading man had looked something like Pinker.

In the morning they watched their man leave his cabin and they tailed him to the saloon and heard him greeted by name by the half-breed barman, who even called him 'mister'. In black broadcloth the feller did look like a mister at that. He was greying, and heavily plump, wore fluffy sideburns and carried himself with importance.

Rimrock was quick to note, however, that the man's gun-rig appeared to be oldish and well-worn. But well looked after also, the heavy Colt hung low, the holster tied to the meaty thigh with a whang-string.

Now he looked like a businessman maybe. Outside the law somehow in all probability, living in a place like this. But to Rimrock, who knew his business, the feller looked also like a retired gunslinger who still kept practising. The thought never entered

Rimrock's head that he mightn't be able to take the feller after all.

The feller started playing a sort of desultory poker with an old goat who looked like a retired judge. To Rimrock's mind most judges, retired or otherwise, were as bent as battered running-irons. Rimrock had a few words with his partner, who nodded, and they walked over to the table and the game and asked if they could take a hand.

At least Pinker asked, calling the two older folk 'gentlemen', beaming on them as if they were his long-lost cousins. They said it was a friendly game they often had but the two young men were welcome to join them.

"Small stakes," said the fancy man.

"Well . . . " said the judge, sort of hesitating. Maybe he was a high-flyer.

So, although the boys had agreed, Rimrock kept upping things. And the judge cackled and came along. And the fancy man, showing off now, went along also.

The place began to fill up. At the next table a big man who looked like some kind of enforcer watched them closely. Glances seemed to pass between him and the fancy feller, although they had only nodded to each other first off.

A few other folks spoke in passing, but nobody made a fuss. Rimrock wondered how popular fancy-man was with these young people, most of whom looked like walking ragbags. Except the pistoleros, who didn't bother anybody but had about them an air of quiet confidence.

Rimrock noted that nobody joined the big man at the adjoining table. He noted that the big man wore his gun low and sort of glowered as if he figured he might pick a fight with somebody some day.

He was no lawman though, that was for sure. A lawman in this burg would be like a violet in a thunderstorm, wilting — or dead. Unless the gink was incognito. So what could he do — whatever?

So Rimrock pulled his wheeze.

"Let me see the other card," he said sharply and he pointed a finger at fancy-man, at fancy-man's cards.

The man bridled, said, "I don't know what you mean," and turned his card up.

"That ain't the one," said Rimrock. "Think you're mighty slick, don't you? And you are, I'll give you that. You got rid o' the one I meant all right. But I been watching you, man, and what you're doing ain't right."

"Are you accusing me o' cheating?"

"Somep'n like that." Maybe he has been cheating after all, reflected Rimrock with sardonic amusement.

The man moved his chair back. "Hold it," said Rimrock. "We'll settle this outside fair an' square. Nobody cheats on me an' gets away with it."

"Nobody calls me a cheat and gets away with it," countered fancy-man.

They both rose. The judge was making noises, protesting maybe. They didn't pay him any attention.

"Your friend stays out of it," said fancy-man.

"He will."

Then they were out on the street and facing each other and there were no more preliminaries.

Fancy-man worked like a pro. He got his gun out as slick as a fast cat on a greasy pole. But then he didn't seem to lift it quickly enough, like he had the rheumatics in his arm or something.

Rimrock had his trigger cut off and used his hammer. Two shots close together and both of them placed in the full of the feller's big chest. Knocking him backwards. Legs kicking and boots banging and then the whole bulk sprawled and supine as the echoes faded away.

But then somebody screamed and Rimrock, still with his smoking gun in his fist, was walking towards Pinker and the big man. The watcher. Both him and Pinker sort of isolated on the edge of the boardwalk.

And then the bigger man was on his

14

knees and grasping his belly. Trying to hold his own bloody intestines as they spilled from the long gash Pinker had ripped in him.

Rimrock saw the life fade from the man's eyes, and the body pitched forward to lie face down at his feet. Pinker said, "I guess he was supposed to look out for that other feller." Wiping his bloodstained blade on his own pants and inspecting its shine before pushing it back in its sheath in back of his belt.

3

PINKER said the town was called Payton. It wasn't much of a place. No better and no worse than the other towns Rimrock had seen while engaged on this job.

And this, when they found their man, was to be the third of the four-part job. Rimrock hadn't done a four-part job before. They usually came just singly, or maybe one led to another sort of, if there were more complications for instance. You had to cover your backs all the time, 'take care of eventualities'. He'd heard Pinker say that once, his very words, the goddam *educated* fancypants!

This time Pinker had done his homework, or said he had. He had been in Payton before, if only briefly, and he thought he had seen the man they were after before. A sort of high

16

muck-a-muck, a big fat fish in a small puddle.

"You point him, I'll take him," said Rimrock.

"First things first," said Pinker enigmatically. Smart. He was beginning to get on Rimrock's nerves a bit. This 'big job' was like wine to Pinker. He was becoming intoxicated by it.

It would soon be dark. During this kill-for-hire go-down they had not yet done an operation by night. "I ain't tired," said Rimrock.

"Me neither," said Pinker. Nothing more. They rode into the town in silence.

But then in main street as the come-evening lights began to blossom Pinker chuckled and said, "I met me a leetle gal here. I wonder if she is still around."

"We ain't got time for dalliance," said Rimrock.

"Oh, I dunno. Under the circumstances, y'know. Women are just naturally talkative. And handled the

17

right way they can be a valuable source of information. Whether or not, there are many ways to make a woman talkative. Forthcoming, y'know." At the end Pinker's voice had sunk to a husky whisper.

"Yeh, I'll bet," said Rimrock.

They had some drinks and some chow in the saloon and Pinker kept his eyes open but didn't see anybody he recognized. They sat unobtrusively at a table in a corner.

The saloon was clean, discreetly lighted, a congenial place better than Rimrock had expected it to be. The hooch was pretty good; and the grub.

Rimrock sat even more in the shadows than Pinker did, didn't want folks to notice his *scalded* visage. And both of the boys kept their heads bent well over their plates as they enjoyed their meal.

Steak grilled in spices and oil with onions; spinach, lima beans and baby potatoes boiled and whole in a covered dish on the side so they could help themselves, the steam rising as they lifted the lid and scooped away with the spoon. Following this, apple and plum cake, sourdough bread with lashings of butter and as much coffee as they could drink poured from a tall hot jug with a white cloth over it to keep the flies out.

They had some stogies and some cold beer and a few more shots of whisky that went down better now than it did the first time.

Rimrock, who was a bit of a booze-fancier, had said he didn't know where some of the Western saloon-keepers got their rotgut. It was the most horrible mash scrapings you could taste. You had to throw it down, preferably not letting it touch the tongue and then wait for the bite in the throat and the belly. Some of 'em put gunpowder in it, he said.

He pronounced this particular mash as better than some, good as some, not a lot worse than others.

"Well, don't get soused on the stuff," Pinker told him.

"I ain't about to do that," said Rimrock.

Truth was, Pinker had never seen his partner worse for any kind of hooch, and his face was never any redder than it was before, no matter how much the runt imbibed.

Rimrock had some funny ways all right, and lately the two of them didn't exactly seem to be seeing eye to eye all the time. But getting drunk so that he couldn't do his work right wasn't one of the runt's little idiosyncracies. Rimrock was all pro, and that was something.

"There she is," said Pinker suddenly and his pale blue eyes seemed to light, even to bug a little.

"What?" Rimrock was startled.

"The gal I told you about."

Rimrock followed the direction of his pard's gaze and saw the girl come from the direction of the kitchen, the door of which was at the end of the bar. She was dark and plump and walked with a little jiggle.

Some of the men spoke to her but none of them reached out to touch her, or get in her way.

Rimrock and Pinker had watched a boy, Indian-like, serving table, and nobody else. The boy, sullen, had served them.

"Mebbe she's the cook," said Rimrock.

"Last time I see'd her she was no cook," said Pinker. He sniggered. "She could mix things well an' she could boil up a storm but she didn't use no knives, forks an' spoons."

The girl didn't glance in their direction. She disappeared through the batwings. By craning his neck Pinker could see her in the street.

"I think I know where she's going," he said. "I'll mosey down there in a mite."

"I'll come with you," said Rimrock.

The street was bright now with light streaming from doors and windows in the warm night. Horses were being reined in. There were more folks on foot in the street and many of them

21

entered the saloon.

Pinker did not see the man he had thought to see, that he might pick as the man they were after.

"I'll go after that gal," he said at length.

Rimrock just tagged along and his taller partner made no formal objection, just gave him one of those sly looks which might have meant a lot and might have meant nothing at all. Rimrock, taciturn as usual, grinned at him with snaggle teeth in boiled red face.

4

IN the starlight they reached a building on the edge of town that looked as if it were ruined, except that a light shone dimly in its interior.

They picked their way through assorted debris and climbed on to a sagging porch. The door sagged so much too that Pinker had difficulty in lifting the latch.

Not knowing what to expect, Rimrock already had his gun out. Pinker didn't bother. The door creaked in a ghostly way as he pushed it open, and then they were in the dim interior. A yellow glow shone palely and, as if smokily, ahead of them.

"The place is even worse than when I last saw it," whispered Pinker.

Rimrock cursed softly as he almost fell over a chair, leaning with one broken leg. They turned a corner with Pinker still leading the way. And ahead of them was a door slightly ajar and it was from this gap that the light streamed.

Pinker made one long step forward and pushed the door open.

Looking past his partner, Rimrock saw the girl. Had a better look at her, under the yellow light as she was, than he had had in the saloon.

She was stripped down to shirtwaist and shift and her feet were bare. She had a voluptuous figure and a plump, pretty face with dark eyes, wide and startled now below the wealth of black hair.

Pinker moved further into what was obviously the kitchen, and smelled that way too, stale. Rimrock moved in beside his pard and the girl said:

"You!"

She was looking straight at Pinker and now there was fear in her eyes. That look was unmistakable.

"Where's your aunt?" Pinker asked.

"She died some months ago. What do you want?"

"I might want you, honey. How about that?"

"I'm not the way I used to be."

"We'll . . . " began Pinker. And Rimrock butted in.

"What were you doin' in the saloon, missy?"

She stared at him as if she had only just spotted him and she said, "I work there."

"What do you do?"

"I'm the cook."

"We had a meal. Grilled steak and the rest. An' apple an' plum cake. Did you do that?"

"I did."

"It was prime," said Rimrock.

Pinker had been looking from one to the other of them, and now he said, "Ain't that nice? Now can we get down to business?"

He moved closer to the girl. Rimrock moved over to the side to watch them both and he saw that Pinker wore that charming smile of his. But his strange eyes were as pale as a snake's.

Pinker's smile faded and then there was death in his handsome face and, subtly, it was not handsome any more, it was evil. And his voice when he spoke again was dull, the words spoken as if by rote.

"We're lookin' for that ol' jasper who used to look after you . . . Before you got respectable I mean. I disremember the man's name."

That sentence is a lie, Rimrock thought. But he didn't interrupt. And Pinker went on. Asking the crucial question now. And the girl's eyes flickered. But she didn't look directly at either of the two men now.

"I don't know what you mean, who . . . ?"

Rimrock reached out and slapped her on the face. Not particularly hard, but hard enough to rock her head a bit, set her hair tumbling.

"Don't lie to me, you little bitch."

She raised her hand to her cheek,

partially obscuring her face. Her dark eyes were enormous and they were deadly scared, shifting like an animal's in a trap.

"If you mean Trailer, he isn't old."

"That's the feller," said Pinker and he shot a glance at Rimrock as if to add I was right all along you see. Aloud he remarked, "He seemed old to me. An old fart who liked to dandle a pretty young gal on his knee."

"He left," the girl said. "I don't know where he is."

"We didn't see him around," said Rimrock, though he wouldn't have known the feller anyway. But he knew Pinker hadn't spotted the man or they wouldn't be here now.

Rimrock balled his fist and pushed it forward in a swift short-arm jab that caught the girl full in the mouth.

She was propelled backwards violently into the dirty yellow sink behind her, beneath the window with the tattered curtains.

Her eyes turned up in their sockets

and blood burst from her shattered mouth and trickled down her chin. She began to sag downwards. The sink did not hold her.

Pinker moved in. And Rimrock said, "Let her be. That won't do it. She's shocked. You'll get nothin'. Mebbe she knows nothin' anyway. Mebbe she's tellin' the truth an' that feller is gone. Leave her to me an' I'll find out."

He had spoken rapidly. Now he looked straight into his partner's face as he measured out his last words.

"Go out, friend, an' leave us be."

Pinker's reactions had always been completely unpredictable. That was the way he played everything. That was one of the things that made him so murderously dangerous. But all he said now, with sardonic undertones, was, "All right, friend."

And he turned and left the kitchen, even closed the door behind him.

How had the girl — and her mysterious aunt, now deceased — let this place get in such a state?

She was sitting on the floor. Rimrock bent, grabbed her arm and lifted her, propped her against the sink. He bent closer and looked into her face.

Her mouth was already beginning to swell and blood coated her chin. Her eyes began to focus again and they were full of unholy terror.

"Are you listening to me?" Rimrock asked.

She tried to find words but couldn't utter them. Her lips moved, writhed. Fresh blood ran down her chin.

"He's crazy, y'know," said Rimrock. "He'll kill you. And he'll do it slowly, make no mistake about that. Tell me about that man, what's-his-name."

"Trailer." She managed to whisper the name.

"Tell me about Trailer an' tell me good."

5

PINKER wasn't in the house any more. When Rimrock got outside Pinker was waiting in the littered yard in the starlight.

He was facing towards the house and he had his gun out and lifted. Pointed straight at the door as Rimrock quit it, walked across the verandah and down the creaking steps.

On hard ground, Rimrock came to a halt. Held his hands away from his sides, the fingers spread.

"Well, if you're gonna do it, do it."

He was poised, ready to move.

"Hell, pardner," said Pinker. "I couldn't shoot you." He sheathed his weapon, stood waiting.

Rimrock tucked his hands in the front of his pants and walked again, approached the taller young man, joined him, said, "That feller's still in town all right. He was rich, then he lost it all. A ranch, everything. The girl didn't seem to know how or why, but that ain't important to us, is it?"

"I guess not."

"He's sick now, had a heart attack. He's lying up in a back room above the saloon and there's a backstairs. I'll take him like I said I would." Rimrock gave a little snort. "I would've liked it a different way, the jasper standin' on his own feet f'instance. But I've got no option, have I? And the job has got to be done."

"You go ahead an' do it then." Pinker jerked a thumb, sniggered. "How about her?"

"I left her. She won't move. I'll do the job an' then we'll get outa this town."

"All right."

The saloon was full of people, and more on the street in the balmy, starlit night, the lights streaming so that the moon, hiding behind scudding clouds, was not needed.

The saloon seemed to burst its doors with noise.

Rimrock found the door to the backstairs on the latch. Pinker and he hadn't seen a soul out back but the noise reached them like the chatter and rumble of an impending storm.

Rimrock didn't see anybody on the stairs or in the passage above, where the noise from below came to him more clearly. Men and women shouting, a piano jangling and somebody trying to sing. He drew his gun.

The door Rimrock needed was slightly ajar. With his free hand, he pushed it a bit further without a sound and slipped through.

The curtains were open and it was lighter in here than in the passage which only had a small window at the end and no lamp burning.

The sleeping figure in the bed was easy to see and did not stir.

Rimrock padded to the side of the bed, moved to the head and looked down at the sleeping form. The breathing was light, but breathing there was.

A gaunt face, straggly greying hair. A big body under the bedclothes. But supine, defenceless. Rimrock sheathed his gun, took out his knife.

Rimrock reached down and swiftly yanked the pillow from beneath the head. The man made a sound as his head fell back. Rimrock clamped the pillow down on the upturned face.

The body beneath the bedclothes began to writhe and sounds came from beneath the pillow. Rimrock used the knife as a dagger and plunged it up and down, up and down with all his force.

He left the pillow as it was and quitted the room. He didn't see a soul and Pinker was waiting with the horses. They mounted up and rode away.

Pinker halted at the tumbledown frame house and, before Rimrock could say anything by way of expostulation, spoke up himself. "I'm gonna have myself a quick time with that gal. I guess you left her in good condition, huh?"

"As good as could be expected."

"You want some as well then?"

"No. And we haven't got time. That old jasper might be found quickly."

"So? Who's to know we've bin there anyway?" said Pinker and he started to walk.

Rimrock sat his horse, turned him around to face back towards town. He listened, watched. The lights shone. The noise continued, nothing strange about it.

Pinker was quicker than Rimrock had expected and mounted up again as the smaller man turned his horse about, the beast momentarily fractious, prancing. Pinker said, "Pity about that gel. She sure knows how to pleasure a man and she tried particularly hard. Sort of make amends I guess 'cos she wasn't cooperating with me in the first place. It was her last go-down, pore bitch."

The message was plain. "You had

to do it, didn't you?" Rimrock said tonelessly.

"She knew us."

"Lots of folks know us. And, like I've said before, we ain't incognito." Rimrock snorted. It wasn't a humorous sound. "Maybe we ought to tie kerchiefs over our faces to disguise ourselves."

"You'd need a bag over your head with two holes in it," Pinker said.

Rimrock laughed harshly, almost immoderately. He could see that Pinker didn't know that he had actually made a joke. His only mirth was glee at misery.

6

COMING out of Digger's Place, he didn't pay much heed to the two men approaching the saloon, hobble-heeling across the pocked, hard-baked street.

They were young saddle-tramps, he thought, and strangers to him. He noticed that the taller of the two was swinging a shotgun negligently at his side. The other one was little more than a runt and badly needed a shave. His face looked burned-red by the sun.

It was the taller who queried, "Mr Renvane?" his smile matching the tone of his voice. He was clean-shaven, a handsome boy.

"I'm Renvane." Maybe they need a job, he thought. But I've got nothing for them right now.

He had one foot on the sidewalk.

The other on the sod. The tall one with the shotgun raised the weapon hip-high, tilting the twin snouts. Was still smiling when he let off both barrels.

Renvane felt as if he were hit by a giant clawed hand, the great fingers clawing as they pushed. A great wind carried him backwards across the splintered boardwalk and through the batwings, his heels coming down then, scraping the boards.

The two wooden wings swung violently, but they were stout and heavy, built to withstand the onslaughts of drunken cowboys; and they soon stilled.

In the saloon one woman screamed. Men shouted.

The two outside had left their horses at a hitching rack on the other side of the street from Digger's Place and outside a dry goods store. They trotted across, mounted-up, set the beasts at a gallop as they left town.

A town called Lobo Peaks which had shootings and fights but nothing to bring death to anyone. Except for a mule-skinner who had recently been kicked in the head by one of his own charges and brained to oblivion.

There hadn't been a real stand-up gunfight for a while. There was nobody hereabouts who could actually be called a *pistolero*. There had been no cold-blooded murder since a visiting drummer had been knifed for his poke, a mystery that had never been solved. And that had been almost five years ago.

But now there had not only been cold-blooded murder but what seemed like an execution. And for what gain?

Renvane, middle-aged and tubby businessman, had been a well-liked character. Now he was hardly recognizable, his body blown to ribbons, his face suffused with blood and a terrible blank staring look in his eyes.

"Cover him, for Godsakes," said somebody, and this was done.

Shots sounded outside, the snapping of handguns like a mockery after the shotgun's boom. And no echoes now.

Two men had gotten outside quickly. But, returning, they said the killers were out of range.

"Get the sheriff," said somebody.

"We hafta get after them bastards," said somebody else.

A woman was weeping quietly in a corner, two men comforting her. She was a slattern, but Renvane had been kind to her.

He had been kind to most everybody, if an astute man in business and not one to waste his time with fools.

More men were moving into the street. Others didn't seem to know what to do, just stared at the dusty tarp that covered a dead friend.

There were shouts from outside. Bootheels sounded louder. A man at the window said it was the law.

A big man entered. Carrying his bulk well, moving swiftly on small feet.

Sweeping old-fashioned black moustache, with his plump florid features and dark looks, made him appear at times Mexican.

A visiting breed, Anglo on one side, had called him 'greaser' and had been put down immediately. Had a broken jaw inexpertly wired by a drunken hack and now went by the handle of Crook-face to the continued amusement of his pure-Indian kinfolk.

Crook-face had vowed vengeance on Sheriff Jim Linlatter but hadn't actually been seen in this territory for some time.

Linlatter looked down at the bulging tarp. Blood was already beginning to seep into the floorboards around it, clotting the sawdust that the swamper had thrown down but a few hours before.

It was barely noon and the sun was high. All the windows were open to let in the breeze, though there wasn't much of that. It had been a piteous time to die.

The sheriff bent and lifted the top end of the tarp and looked into the staring face. He closed the lids over the staring eyes.

"Anybody seen Johnny?"

Johnny was Linlatter's deputy. Seemed like nobody had seen him.

"He said he was calling in here this morning," the sheriff remarked.

A man came through the batwings towing a redheaded boy about eight years old.

"Get 'im outa here," said the barman.

"Lenny saw 'em," said the man excitedly. "He saw them two killers."

Linlatter covered the body completely with the tarp and turned away.

"Come outside with me, son," he said to the wide-eyed boy. His hand gently on the thin shoulder. Some folks following. Others still hardly moving, bemused by death so quickly come, so violently.

"The tall one looked at me an' pulled out his gun," Lenny said. "But the little 'un sort of moved his horse forward. He said 'Hallo, son' and they

41

went on. They wuz goin' pretty fast."
His voice got important. "Then all I
could see was their dust."

"But you got a pretty good look at
'em, huh?"

"Sure."

"Go on."

"The one was little and looked as if
he might be trying to grow a beard."

His face was very red but not by sun,
the boy thought — by something else.

The other one had been just the
opposite, sort of, and maybe younger.
He had been handsome. But the way
he had looked at the boy had made
Lenny shudder. And the way he had
pulled his gun. Lenny hadn't expected
that. He had heard the shotgun . . .

But he hadn't expected the young
feller to pull a gun on him, nossir. Even
now he seemed surprised at that.

★ ★ ★

"I don't shoot children," said Rimrock.
"I do what I have to do an' then I

42

hightail. No more, no less."

"That kid got a good look at us," said Pinker.

"So? We ain't hard to identify."

"You got a point there." Pinker looked at his partner speculatively. "Well, mebbe I was a mite hasty at that. But I don't like you getting in my way. Hell, I could've shot you."

"Horse-shit! You could've missed."

"I didn't miss that old jasper."

"A shotgun!"

"I could've fazed him with a handgun had I wanted. You didn't have to do a goddam thing, and it was a certain kill. Nobody could've lived through that blast."

"I've seen it happen."

"What do you want to do? Go back and do him over again?"

"That's an interesting suggestion. But, nah — I'll pass."

"That cheeky-faced kid had eyes like a bluejay," said Pinker.

"I swear," said Rimrock. "You're the damndest."

7

THAT was the fourth one. The last one.

They had a good start on anybody, hadn't seen any sign of pursuit. In the main they had avoided habitations, but stopped at last at a sort of way station to pick up supplies. Pinker was as charming as all hell to the middle-aged couple who kept the place.

But he didn't shoot 'em afterwards and he and his partner went on their way merrily. And Rimrock asked, "What was that town called, did y' say?"

"Lobo Peaks."

"Looked same as everyplace else to me."

"Yeh, you've hit the bull there I guess, pardner. And all these little towns look alike as well. And the folk — the folk you an' me had to do I mean — ain't they sort of alike as well?"

"I guess I know what you're getting at. Middle-aged quiet folk in quiet towns. What better place to hide than a quiet town, settle, become part of the community?"

"But why?"

"Don't ask me why. I don't want to know why. I'm getting the *dinero* and the rest . . . "

"The rest! You certainly like your work don't you, pizen?"

"I've had worse. I've choked on dust on the ass-ends of herds of stinking beef an' I've eaten wormy gruel in a jail cell. This'll do me. Why, you suddenly, getting religion or somep'n?"

"Nope."

Rimrock had sprung from a clan of border scum, had had no proper upbringing and no education at all, couldn't even write his own name. Like the rest of his breed had lived by thieving, pillaging. And by violence.

Always by violence. Most of his clan had died violent deaths, in gang fighting, at the end of hangropes, blasted by the guns of vigilantes or law.

Pinker had never talked about his past life. But he could read and write very well. And he sure as hell could talk when he had to. A handsome and charming young man, he could pass in any company. And this was something that Rimrock couldn't do.

Didn't want to, Rimrock told himself. Fat cats with polish and loud voices, how he hated 'em! He would like to kill 'em all. But cleanly.

But Pinker would like to kill everybody and *anybody*, I swear, thought Rimrock. And he wondered why Pinker was like that. (Maybe he was just plumb crazy!) And why he had picked such as he (saddle-tramp Rimrock) as a partner?

They had met in a saloon, as simple as that. During a game of five-card stud Pinker had pinned a jasper's hand to a table with his long-bladed knife which he called a stiletto. Had said the man was cheating, though Rimrock hadn't seen evidence of that.

The feller had certainly been winning, though. Nobody else had said a hoot. And Rimrock and Pinker had taken most of the money and breezed.

And they both had connections. And they used them.

They earned good money. Neither of them had thought about stopping yet, settling down.

Pinker will never stop, Rimrock thought. He is living now, really living; this is what he wants. As for Rimrock himself, he went from day to day and didn't think about the morrow unless, because of business in hand, he just had to.

★ ★ ★

Johnny was Sheriff Jim Linlatter's young deputy. Real name actually Juan.

He had left the law office that

morning to go to the edge of town to visit his ma. It wasn't too far and he had been walking.

The old lady had a trap and a pony. Maybe they had gone for a spin.

Linlatter wanted Johnny for a posse. But finally the posse had had to leave without him. Picked men, but not actually gunslingers. All of them good with long guns as most Westerners seemed to be. But not a one that could be called a *pistolero*, except the sheriff himself.

Johnny was good. He practised. But he wasn't here right now and they didn't see him on the way out which was unfortunately in the opposite direction to the frame house where Johnny's ma lived.

Half-a-dozen men counting Linlatter. And the redheaded boy Lenny pointing the way, running ahead a bit till his ma called him to heel.

In the direction taken by those two killers.

After that it was just the trail and

keeping to it. And those two boys had cut off, as they would have, and hadn't followed anything that you could actually call a trail.

The posse had an old tracker, who was good with a rifle too, an old Indian fighter. Finally he had to say, "Those two boys are professional I guess. We ain't gonna catch up with 'em."

He sounded grieved. But they went on and they tried. They saw places unfamiliar to some of them. They called in on a small ranch and a smallholding and a soddie where a wild hermit lived. Nobody had seen two strange riders. A lean young man and a runty one with a very red face.

The posse turned back, aching, their horses not too good. "I'll put the word out," said Sheriff Jim Linlatter sombrely.

8

FULL name Juan Augusto Guillermo Henrique Tortuga. Johnny to his friends, both Anglo and Mexican.

He was proud of being called Johnny by his friends but he was proud of his other names also. His mother would never let him forget that he should be proud of his heritage. She claimed to belong to a high-born family who had prospered in Durango. But Johnny had never met any relatives from there and did not worry that he should.

He honoured his mother, was sure he would never do anything to dishonour her. It could be said that the two people in this world that he honoured most — loved — were first of all his mother, and then his chief. His great Anglo friend, Sheriff Jim Linlatter.

Johnny was proud to be part of the

town of Lobo Peaks. And a law deputy no less. This was what he had wanted, and this was what he had got.

His father had been killed by two thieves who had broken into the small store during the night. When surprised by the owner, they had stabbed him to death. Little Juan's father had been stabbed dozens of times all over his body in a frenzied attack.

Juan was an only son, which was pretty rare in Mexican families. But his mother had not married again. With her child, she had travelled from the border and across Texas, selling her wares from a covered wagon, a conglomeration of household utensils and work clothes and farming implements, but never any items of offence. She became well-known at the ranches, the smallholdings, the small towns that clustered on the Texas border-lands which rolled away from the Rio Grande.

She got rheumatism, though, and travelling did not help this at all. She

51

ATCHISON LIBRARY
401 KANSAS
ATCHISON, KS 66002

finally settled in her frame house on the edge of Lobo Peaks, where she was already known and welcome. She didn't actually run a store then but sold her wares from the house that was open to all.

She had suitors. But she didn't choose one. She brought up her boy lovingly but strictly. He did odd jobs for the sheriff, who was his mother's friend, had once been thought to be one of her suitors.

And finally Juan (Johnny) became deputy to the man he admired so much and always called 'Sheriff Jim'.

He hated the kind of folk Sheriff Jim hated, the kind of folk that had killed his father, the mindless scum who preyed on the West. He wanted to exterminate them. He taught himself expertise with weapons. Sheriff Jim helped him greatly.

He knew that in her heart of hearts his mother was not happy with what he did. If Juan had not been under the wing of an old friend, she would have objected strongly.

Luckily, Lobo Peaks was a fairly peaceable town . . .

But then that thing happened.

That morning Johnny's mother's sickness of the bones was particularly bad, probably because she had been lifting stock herself instead of waiting for Johnny to do it for her, or calling in a kid off the streets maybe.

Johnny chided her. He was very much the man of the house now. It was a hot morning and he said the sun would do her good. He took her for a ride in the gig to their favourite picnic spot.

He said that things were quiet in town and that Sheriff Jim wouldn't need him. In his anxiety for his mother in her pain he forgot that he had promised to meet his chief in Digger's Place come noon.

He and his mother took their noontide repast in a grassy wooded draw by a shallow stream that burbled over white pebbles. They drank cordial that the woman made herself. Their faces shaded by big hats, they drowsed in the sun.

Later, Johnny dropped his mother at the house and walked quickly into the centre of town. His mother said she felt much better and she would stretch her legs looking after the gig and the horse.

There was something wrong with the town. It was not the same as it had been when he left it in the early morning. He sensed the difference. The main street was deserted. He caught a glimpse of a man in an alley who then disappeared.

Then Johnny reached the saloon and the ominous buzz of voices reached out to him. He walked into it. He walked into everything.

He got his horse almost right away and he rode out after the posse.

He met them, and they were returning. While Johnny and his mother had been enjoying their picnic they had seen grazing cows and one coyote and a line-riding single cowboy in the distance through the entrance of the draw and between a gap in the sparsely spaced trees.

They had also seen two riders going away from the direction of Lobo Peaks. Johnny had made a joke about those two. Had said they had overstayed their time with a couple of girls in town and were on their way back to one of the ranches, afraid of being canned for their tardiness. Waddies were a dime a dozen after all.

But those two could have been the couple who had killed Rafe Renvane. The time had been right.

"Which way were they headed?" Jim Linlatter asked.

Johnny pointed. "I brought those two to mind while I was riding to find you. And I wondered . . . "

"Goddammit," put in the old tracker explosively. "I led you wrong."

"We don't know," said the sheriff. "Those two Johnny and his mom saw could've been a couple of tardy cowboys after all. You did your best, old-timer."

They were sad and tired men. Plodding, heads down, their mounts seemed to match their masters' moods.

It was full dark and there was a pale moon and a few stars. After the sun of the day it seemed a gloomy night. And now would be the time of the undertaker and a funeral would have to be arranged. And the law had plans to make.

★ ★ ★

It was pretty well known now that before Jim Linlatter became sheriff of Lobo Peaks he had been a Texas Ranger. He had done his stint and then, like many others, had moved on. Not everybody liked the discipline of the Rangers, and Jim was a free-wheeling sort of gent.

During his Ranger days he used to visit Lobo Peaks quite frequently on his off-days and was sparking a female there, Bella, whom he subsequently married. It was because of Bella that he decided to settle in the town, though not as a lawman. Bella certainly hadn't contemplated that.

But Jim was what he was and couldn't change and as sheriff he would at least be his own boss. Bella was a fine woman very much in love with her man. She went along. She was a lovely woman and had fought off many suitors because she was so attached to her ailing widowed mother. Folks said it would be a sin if that fine woman became an old maid, and the bullying she took from that old lady was something terrible at times.

Bella's meetings with Jim had to be surreptitious. But then the loud-mouthed old lady, who some said was slated to last till Doomsday, died very suddenly. Choked on some prime steak.

Bella, working as a seamstress and also cooking for other folk, had always seen that her mother had the best she could get for her. The old woman, though bedridden with some complaint of the bones and muscle, ate like a young and greedy horse and hastily as if somebody aimed to take it away from her. And this was her undoing.

After the funeral and a period of mourning which Bella insisted upon, she was free to marry her Jim. Her father, a chuck-wagon jockey, had died in a cattle stampede. Bella was the only offspring and, it seemed, one of the few things he actually shared with his wife, who had been taken poorly a few years before he was killed.

And tragedy seemed to dog that small family.

Bella wanted a child. The local doctor told her it would be a chancy thing. With all her fetching and carrying for her mother, and the actual lifting of that heavy woman as well, there had been strain to her insides. Neither Bella or Jim understood this very well.

The doc said maybe if they waited . . .

Bella wasn't getting any younger. Jim

said they shouldn't take a chance. But, even so, it happened . . .

Bella died in childbirth. The child too, the child that had been her heart's desire. Something small and gentle to look after. It had been her wish, her chance . . .

It was something for which Jim Linlatter would never forgive himself and often he went riding alone without telling anybody where he was going, which was not really a good thing for a lawman to do. But the townsfolk understood his moods. He was their Jim, *their lawman*, and there wasn't a better one.

Now he had Johnny Tortuga. Some of the folks had been dubious about Johnny at the start. But there weren't many of that kind now. Johnny was a feature of the town. Hell, he was a town boy! His mother was widely respected. Johnny could take care of himself better than most, was a fine back-up for a favourite sheriff.

And when Jim wasn't here Johnny

was always at hand. Smiling under his black pencil moustache in his handsome face. He could have been Jim's nephew. Courteous, watchful.

Sometimes Jim didn't even tell Johnny when he was going on one of his lonely ride-abouts. Johnny was surprised when, not long after the posse returned after its fruitless chase of Rafe Renvane's killers, his chief said he was going out alone. He had something to do, he said, he'd be back as soon as he could.

"All right, Sheriff Jim," Johnny said. He wondered whether his chief knew something he didn't. About those killers maybe. But he didn't ask.

Linlatter was away overnight, did not return in the morning. And on that morning Johnny Tortuga had a couple of visitors in the law office.

They were two hard-bitten Anglos, still pretty young, but older than the Mexican deputy. They had heard about Sheriff Linlatter, had expected to see him. They eyed Johnny a bit askance, were, it seemed, suspicious of him, wary.

"Where's your badge?" one of them demanded.

Johnny didn't usually wear it around town. He took it from his vest pocket, pinned it on.

They had come right to the office, hadn't learned that there had recently been a killing in Lobo Peaks. It was just a coincidence. Or was it?

But their explanation was watertight. They were after two men who had killed a man and his wife at a ranch down on the border. They were the dead man's nephews.

They had gotten a line on the men they were pretty sure were responsible for the murders and had trailed them in this direction. Young men. A tall fancypants and a runt with a very red face. They had no names.

Johnny told them he had no names either. He told them of the killing of Rafe Renvane and of how a local boy, diminutive Lenny, had seen the two men ride out of town.

Lenny's description matched that given by the two visitors. The two riders were all ears now, no uncertainty in their manner towards the young Mexican deputy any more.

"Those two bastards must be on some sort of a killing spree," said one.

Johnny thought it was probably more sinister than that, but he didn't say so. He asked, "Did they rob those folk?"

"Not that we could find out." The talkative rider had a wall eye and an incipient beard. His companion, thin to the point of being cadaverous, had a doleful expression and didn't say much.

"You think Sheriff Linlatter has a line on those two now?" the talky one asked.

Johnny didn't quite know what to say to that. But his humour was not devious. After a slight pause, he confessed, "I dunno."

"So he left you to watch the town?"

"Somep'n like that."

"That figures," put in the silent one surprisingly.

"Yeh," agreed the other. "But you would've thought he'd taken a posse with him like before."

"You haven't got a posse," said Johnny Tortuga.

"We had one. And law. But our man said that he was goin' outside his jurisdiction."

"Idle, fat-assed bastard," said the silent partner explosively.

Johnny said, "Maybe the sheriff thinks he can do better on his own this time. He's a professional. I reckon he can handle those two if he gets the chance."

"We heard he was good," said the talky one. The other seemed to have sunk once more into a doleful stupor, leaning like a starving crane. The talky one went on, "But it seems to me those two killers operated like professionals as well. Executioners. Hired guns. Unless maybe they had some wayback grudge against your man and ours. And they killed our aunt too, just for the hell and to stop her alarm. The man was shot. The woman was knifed."

"Can you help?" asked the cadaverous one, awakening once more.

Johnny had his orders, his duties. He had to do what was best for his town. He said, "I've to stay here. I'm the only law right now."

9

HE looked out across the great land. It was not late in the morning and the sun was not too hot.

He could see the heat-haze burgeoning out in the far horizon like pale blue smoke. Still. But thickening even as he watched.

The land in between seemed limitless though, brown and green and gold, bathed in the sun, the grass rippling in a slight breeze which, sheltered by the house, he could not feel at all.

The breeze made shadows move across grass as if momentarily a huge hand, sweeping slowly, moving indolently, had passed above and over and across the great earth.

Over to the right of him as he turned his head slowly he could see the rippling lumps of the hills the

Indians had dubbed The Little Ones. And beyond them was the town. But around him, after the outhouses ended, there was only that great space. That great land in which he had been, in which he had grown.

And now his thick hair was grey at the sides and the moustache which had once been so black had silver streaks.

A man could stay here in love and peace and he had done this. But his woman had gone now and there were no children and he was alone, except for during the day when the two hands came out to help him from town. Today was Sunday and, good boys, they would be at the church in the dip.

From here he could not see the church, not even if he walked completely around the house and gazed in all directions. He could only see the cluster of buildings on the edge of town.

He was not a churchgoer and he didn't want to go into town. But he wanted to go *some place*, he surely did. The old restlessness was on him again. He had fought it a long time and thought maybe he couldn't fight it any more.

How many times recently had he stood outside his door and felt like getting his horse? Getting his gear together? Leaving this small spread behind, lock, stock and barrel? Riding out into that wide blue yonder and never looking back.

And he had gotten his horse all right. But then he had ridden out to join the boys or, if he had any free time, had gone to town and sat in the saloon. Had drank, had visited a girl or two, had come home in the misty twilight or in the dark, wobbling in the saddle.

Maybe I'll go into town later today, he thought. He couldn't remember whether he had any chores to do. He had already had breakfast and washed the crockery and left everything tidy. He had never let this place go to pot in any way at all.

He was a disciplined man. A man who held a duty to himself now as he had once held duty as a Texas Ranger. Finally a captain no less; and some folks still called him 'Cap'n'.

He strolled out onto the well-swept yard. He looked towards the edge of town and he thought he saw something moving. The sun was in his eyes now and he shaded them with his hand.

A rider was leaving town and coming in his direction.

Maybe it was one of the boys who had forgotten something on leaving the spread yesterday. A single horseman anyway.

And the lone man, standing, waiting could not think of anybody else who might be visiting him on a Sunday morning.

He moved back to the house, taking his eyes off the approaching horseman. Then, back at the door, he looked out once more. The sun's rays were no problem now. The man and horse were, of course, nearer, clearer to his sight, coming on straight as if heading for this place.

Not one of the boys. Older and heavier than any of those. And the horse not looking too fresh, as it would have done had it just left town. Tired maybe from the weight and the travelling.

The look of the rider became clearer. A figure that looked familiar. But not a familiar town-figure, the watching man thought, memory tugging at him, eluding him; then tugging again stronger, until he could see the face of the rider and the memory burst forth. Startling him. But then, he thought, *pleasing him*.

He started forward. The other man slowed his horse.

"Jim Linlatter."

"Jim Linlatter it is, Cap'n," said the heavy man as he reined in his mount and slid down from the saddle.

★ ★ ★

They sat drinking coffee at the big scrubbed deal table in the neat, spacious kitchen and Linlatter said, "I had a bit of a job to find you. I thought you were still badge-toting. I went to that old town where you used to be. I was told you had gone free-lancing."

"Bounty-hunting you mean."

"If you say so. They still called you 'Cap'n' in that old town, though. They still remembered you, remembered they used to look up to you."

"Folks do still call me 'Cap'n' even hereabouts. But others call me Ed. Or even Mr Gallion. As I remember, Jim, you allus used to call me Ed."

"I guess. I like this place, Ed. How come you finished up here?"

"I got married. She didn't like lawdogging. Bounty-hunting either. I put some cash together, bought this place, and we settled. We didn't have no offspring. She died a year ago, during the winter and that great norther we had, remember? No, it was above a year o' course, wasn't it?"

"It was. And who could forget that winter, huh?"

"Yeh. And I was drunk for a long time after that."

"It figures. But you allus used to be able to hold your liquor, Ed."

"I ain't as young as I used to be."

"Who is?"

"How about you, Jim? You ain't still with the Rangers are you?"

"Hell, no. I'm sheriff of a town called Lobo Peaks down near the border."

"Come to think of it, I did hear you had started badge-toting."

"Beats taking orders I guess. I got married and settled down. My wife died, too."

"Oh, mercy."

They were old friends and it was as if the years had rolled back. They were open with each other. Gallion found himself talking to Jim Linlatter about things that he had bottled inside himself for years. And Jim was just as forthcoming.

But eventually the inevitable question had to be asked and the visitor had been expecting it.

"What brings you here, Jim? Why were you looking for me?"

"I didn't know you had settled. When I found out you had I almost turned back. But one or two folks knew who I was and you might've been told I was around and wonder why I hadn't called on you after all, particularly as I had been asking after you."

"What about?"

"I wanted your help. You might say I was willing to hire you. It's to do with something that might, indirectly, concern us both. But now I figure it mightn't concern you at all, you being settled an' all. So we can forget it and I'll just sit and visit a piece and then go on my way. No harm done and you just like you were before, peaceful an' settled."

"Hell, Jim, I ain't settled," said Ed Gallion caustically.

When they rode, they rode together. But Linlatter said that Gallion would be a fool to leave everything behind him, burn his boats. He might want peace again (what was peace, Gallion asked?), might want to return. This was a nest-egg, a modest one but a fine one ripe for growing.

So they called on the two ranchhands in town. Caught them in their after-church repast. And Gallion gave them *carte blanche* to run the spread for him while he was away. He said he'd get in touch from time to time, maybe he'd be back sooner than expected . . .

"Or mebbe I'll be buried elsewhere," he added as he and Linlatter rode on. An afterthought. "And I do mean buried."

He added, "They're good boys, those two. Straight, hard workers, good with stock. They might've been the sons I never had and, if I go, they're welcome to the place."

"They're married, they're settled," said Linlatter. "And I see that one of 'em's got a kid already."

"Maybe, when you get down to the rock-bottom end, that sort of thing has never been for you an me, Jim. We're back on the hootin' trail again like we used to be and we're comfortable with it like four old shoes on an amblin' old jackass."

10

JOHNNY TORTUGA wondered why Sheriff Jim had been so goddam secretive. He had gone away without much to say except to tell his deputy to take care of things, and that went without telling of course. He hadn't given Johnny any inkling of when he would be back. He had seemed hurried, harassed even.

Johnny wondered if this had anything to do with the telegraph messages Sheriff Jim had received of late. Since the murder of Rafe Renvane mostly. Was this trip all about the same thing? What *could* a man think?

Juan Augusto Guillermo Henrique Tortuga was an intelligent young man but he was no soothsayer. He became uncertain and a mite irritable, a cat on hot bricks not knowing which way to dance. His doting ma wondered what in Hades was the matter with him.

He wondered about the two strangers who had called on him and were gone now. He should have caught up with them again and questioned them further. The wall-eyed one and his cadaverous untalkative friend or cousin or whatever.

They had said they were after two men who had killed their aunt and uncle. Two men who had clearly answered to the description, given by the boy Lenny, of the murderers of Rafe Renvane in Lobo Peaks, Johnny Tortuga's town.

The two strangers hadn't known the names of those killers. And Deputy Tortuga hadn't gotten the names of the two strangers and they sure as hell hadn't volunteered any.

Two killings by the same two men. Hired guns? Or were they two people carrying out some kind of vendetta as the two later strangers, wall-eye and lank, were also carrying out now? Those two had looked like hardcases well able to embark on a trail of vengeance and bring it to a bloody conclusion.

I didn't act like a lawman, Johnny thought. A lawman should ask questions. Sheriff Jim always asked questions in that soft drawling voice of his which could turn to steel if needs be. And most times Sheriff Jim got answers.

Johnny thought, would I get answers as easily as Sheriff Jim does?

Of course he wouldn't, couldn't be expected to. To many folks Johnny was the unfledged deputy, certainly no seasoned lawman, and ex-Ranger to boot, like the sheriff.

Sometimes folks — and particularly young rannies riding in from the ranches — decided to try Johnny out. And right now, with the sheriff absent, such folks had a prime opportunity.

Cowboys started to hurraw the saloon. And Johnny was glad of the action.

He hadn't shot anybody yet and didn't aim to unless such a course was advisable. Sheriff Jim had taught him that no lawman should use a gun unless absolutely necessary. But, among his own people Johnny Tortuga was known as a wrestler and fist-fighter of prime excellence.

When he marched into the saloon he wasn't sporting his gun-gear, two guns if he needed them, but had a derringer in back of his belt just in case.

As he came along the street, the sound which he had detected back in the law office had gotten louder. As he swung through the batwings the sound hit him in the face like a large bag of mush flung by a powerful hand.

The place was pretty full. It was difficult to assess right off exactly what was going down. There was turmoil, shouting voices, crashing glass, breaking furniture. Most of the cacophony seemed to be coming from over near the long bar. Older folk were backing away from that area and one of them called, "Here's the depitty."

They didn't balk him. They got out

of his way. One oldster said, "Go get 'em, Johnny."

Another voice echoed, shouting, "Here comes the law depitty." A younger voice, cheerfully mocking.

It came from an appropriately cheerful face which, however, looked now as if it had been recently pushed into a mess of prickly pear, the straw-coloured hair tangled and awry; one wicked eye half-closed; checked shirt torn open to reveal a muscular, hairless chest.

A local ranny called Jingo with whom the Lobo Peaks law had had trouble before. Sheriff Jim had had to pistol-whip him and put him in a cell, letting his rancher boss bail him out come morning. The sheriff had said then he wasn't going to get in a fist-fight with a drunken buck, not at his time of life.

Deputy Tortuga had been elsewhere at the time. Now he welcomed a second chance. Young buck himself, and raring to go, he had been looking for action. He approached Jingo with delight.

Jingo had friends. They had all sort of come in to test the water. Since Jingo had had a run-in with Sheriff Jim Linlatter none of them had tried anything untoward. But they had heard that the fat man was away on a trip and Johnny was in charge. They didn't dislike Johnny. Two of them at least had grown up in the same town with him. But they had a night off and they wanted some fun.

Jingo, as usual, had been the one to start it.

He had spilled stogie-ash into the drink of a harmless middle-aged townie. When the man had objected, Jingo had stamped on his toe with a heavy riding boot. The man had howled and hopped away from the bar. Had been prevented by his friends from drawing a gun. Wouldn't have been a match for Jingo anyway, who was much younger and reputed to be fast with a shooting iron, though nobody had actually seen him use one; not in town anyway.

Cowboys always bragged and showed

off and this bunch were no exception. Townsfolk tolerated them, even enjoyed them sometimes. They were a good source of business. But they shouldn't be allowed to get too uppity. Jim Linlatter had seen to that.

After Jingo had used his stamping-heel, his friends had started jostling other folk at the bar, elbowing them aside yelling for hooch, pretending they were back from a long drive and were spit-dry. But everybody knew there hadn't been a roundup and drive for some time.

A younger townsman had knocked one ranny sprawling and had been set upon by another two.

Others of the younger element of townspeople had joined in and the mélêe had become somewhat indiscriminate.

When the deputy turned up, there was a lull as folks stepped aside, remarking on the fact that he wasn't wearing his usual hardware. Was that wise?

But then Johnny and Jingo were confronting each other and the former asked mildly, "Are you the ringleader then?"

Jingo threw his head back and laughed. Somebody had hit him. In the mêlée, he hadn't been sure who it was. But now here was a foe right in front of him: the one he had been looking for. And so mealy-mouthed too.

Jingo stopped spluttering. "Hallo there, Johnny," he said.

Three pards moved forward. He waved them back. He stared at Johnny out of his one good eye, the other being temporarily on the blink. "What did you call me?"

"I didn't call you anything. I just asked if you were the ringleader?"

"That's the word," carolled Jingo, throwing his head back again. Then looking around him as if in triumph. "Ain't that fancy?"

"Sure is" . . . "yes, suh" . . . "Oh, great day, that's a helluva fancy word all right." Jingo's friends were enthusiastic in their support.

Nobody on the townie side said much. They were wondering what the deputy was going to do about this upstart young cowpusher.

And Jingo asked the question for them. Blinking owlishly. His head on one side now as if wanting to examine Johnny from every angle, as if he had never seen this new deputy before, although once they could have been called friends, had played together as tads.

"And if I am the ringleader, you being so all-fired fancy an' all, what are you going to do about it, my proud bucko?"

His friends applauded noisily. Jingo, too, could talk fancy if he put his mind to it.

"What am I gonna do about it?" echoed Johnny and there was a new tone in his voice now. "I'm gonna take you outside an' beat the tar outa yuh."

"Just you an' me, huh, Johnny?" asked Jingo silkily.

"Yes, *amigo*, just you and me."

"I'm a mite bruised already, Johnny."

"All right, I'll have one hand tied behind my back."

"Like hell you will! Come on!"

Jingo marched straight forward at the deputy. Johnny stood aside to let him by. Then turned and followed him. The rest of the assembled populace streamed behind.

In a matter of seconds the saloon was empty. Even the barman left his post. The old swamper, who liked to sleep after his morning chores were done, came in from his cubbyhole out back and brought up the rear.

It was as if some jungle drums had been beaten, or somebody had seen Indian smoke signals. That hadn't happened for years.

People came into main street from other directions and a sort of ragged ring was made on the baked, dusty, cart-rutted street.

Jingo took off his gun-rig and handed it to one of his pards. Johnny even produced his derringer which had been hidden by the back-flap of his scuffed leather vest.

"Oh, will you look at that?" said Jingo. "What a sneaky character you are, ain't you?"

"But fair," retorted Johnny as they squared up to each other.

11

"SO we've done 'em all now," said Pinker.

He ticked them off on his fingers. Right now he was being as methodical as a bank teller. Rimrock thought he preferred him the other way, reckless and unpredictable. Seemed that, just lately, Pinker was irritating the hell out of him. And Pinker went on, "The first one was at that smallholding. The feller an' the woman."

"You did the woman," said Rimrock.

"So, I did the woman," said Pinker as if that were only a footnote. "Then there was the gamblin' man."

"I set that up. I did that one."

"So you did. But I gutted that friend o' his who was about to backshoot you."

"Granted," said Rimrock sardonically. "*Gracias, amigo.*"

"You're welcome. I remember that one's name. The gamblin' man I mean. It was Doobel. Funny sort of moniker."

"Hell, who remembers names? Dead is dead an' that's the end of it, name an' all. Then the third one . . . "

Pinker interrupted, cut in. He said quickly, "Yes! Then the last one."

"Sure," said Rimrock. He remembered the last one all right. But most of all he remembered the third one. And particularly remembered the dark, plump girl — he had liked her — who had given him the information about the man called Trailer whom they had been looking for.

She had been a good cook. She would never cook again. Pinker had seen to that.

"We've got to wait a while now," said Pinker, "before we go an' pick up the rest of the *dinero*. We don't want anybody following us."

"As far as we know there ain't anybody following us."

"That was the arrangement."

"Since when have you started to stick to arrangements?"

"Since now. Mebbe Callicot thinks we might try an' trace back to the people who wanted the job done in the first place."

"Why would he think that? Why would anybody think that?"

"Why not? Such a big job. The biggest we've ever done. Four-in-one. The biggest anybody's ever done, that we know about anyway. Who else could've tackled it but us? Could you think of anybody else?"

"No."

"All right then. Callicot knows what he's doing. He's got his instructions. He won't hand over the rest of the cash till he's told to. Mebbe he hasn't even got it yet. He recommended us. He knows we're professionals."

"That we are," said Rimrock, coming around partly to his partner's way of thinking now. He (Rimrock), who had always been the cautious one before, had chided Pinker for his reckless carelessness and his bloodlust.

Job done, job done well, he wanted the money, *pronto*, but the hirer, through the link-man Callicot, still held the rest of the deck.

"Where do we go from here then?" Rimrock asked.

"I know a place."

Pinker always seemed to know a place. And the uncertainty was beginning to make Rimrock's red face itch. "All right, bucko, lead me to it."

As they rode, Rimrock scratched.

His own brother had done it to him. With a flaming torch. And they had only, wild kids, been arguing around a bonfire over the sharing of baked potatoes in the heart of the flaming logs. And Rimrock's brother had thrust a spurting red brand into the younger one's face.

Rimrock, called Ben then, had been almost blinded. He had worn steel-rimmed spectacles for a long time. Had left them off as a youth when he first learned to shoot straight and started to perfect his draw.

By that time he was as big as his brother. The wild clan had done nothing to punish the latter. Now Rimrock took it upon himself to do that, to wreak a long-awaited vengeance.

He beat his brother to submission and, as he lay, stamped him.

If Rimrock had a bad face, his brother still had a crooked arm when they met a couple or so years ago. They called it quits. Rimrock had learned since that his brother had been hung down in Sonora but he didn't know whether this was true or not. The clan was split every which way and Pinker was Rimrock's 'family' now.

Some family! Madder than any of the clan had ever been. Rimrock felt like laughing out loud as he scratched. Pinker talked better than any of that lot had done. He could even read and write. He had never attempted to shove a flaming torch in his partner's face but was quite capable of doing so. And worse.

They were travelling now over a flat and arid land. Not long ago they had seen better places. They had killed in better places. Even the outlaw town where Rimrock had stabbed the murder subject in bed had been a better place. A hideout. But they could not have hidden out there. Somebody might have taken umbrage. They hadn't risked having their necks stretched by some of their own kind.

But was Pinker making for a similar place where they could lie low until it was time to move again, to go see the go-between Callicot? But who had Callicot's boss, or bosses, been? It was an intriguing question but Rimrock, all professional again, told himself not to worry about the answer.

They had known Callicot but hadn't used him as a link-man before. He had actually approached them, which was to their credit. And Callicot was a professional too, as tight-mouthed as a pauper's purse.

Rimrock looked behind him. Nothing. All around. The badlands. Only fit for horned toads. And the sun now like a molten ball.

"We could do with some shelter."

"We'll get shelter," Pinker said.

★ ★ ★

The sun was getting up but the false front of the saloon called Digger's Place in the town called Lobo Peaks threw a shade across the street as the two contestants faced each other and began to move in.

They circled each other, their fists up and weaving. Neither had any sort of professional stance. Johnny Tortuga knew that Jingo was an accomplished street fighter and would use every trick in the book. But Johnny had wrestled with his boyhood friends and had been noted for his expertise.

He aimed to get as near as possible to Jingo. Then maybe he could teach that big loudmouth a few tricks, not Anglo-style but Mexican catch-as-catch-can.

Jingo swung at him. Johnny ducked. The blow missed by a small mile. Jingo's one eye was still a bit on the blink from the shenanigans he had been involved in inside the saloon before Deputy Tortuga took a hand.

Johnny swung in closer. Blinking owlishly and with a half-smile on his face, Jingo weaved away. Twisting, he swung again. This time the big fist caught the deputy a glancing blow on his shoulder. Nothing solid. But enough to unsettle him.

The big feller was too eager, though. Swung again, a follow-up blow delivered with the left hand, and that missed entirely. And Jingo was on his opponent. And Johnny grasped him. Seemed suddenly to have hands every place. Swung him. Threw him.

The crowd, up till now single voices yelling for individual champions, let out their first collective shout. Jingo sprawled on the ground. Spat into the swirling cloud of dust.

He reached out for Johnny's dancing leg. Missed it. Right then the deputy could have kicked his opponent's face in. As this was a no-holds-barred street fight nobody would have blamed him, but evidently he didn't mean to play it that way.

He danced away. Had he been fighting a boyhood friend time back, involving them both in a wrestling match, he would have sprung on his man. Locked him. Pinned him to the ground. But, if only partly, he was allowing Jingo to choose his own game.

The big feller took advantage of this. Lurched to his feet more quickly than could have been expected. Charged, bull-like. The crowd created with a roar of enthusiasm, a commodity of which Jingo himself had never been short.

Johnny sidestepped. Using his fist like a hammer, he caught the moving man with a blow to the side of the head. Sent him spinning. But Jingo didn't go down. Shaking his head like an enraged bull. Moving in. Swinging fists in all directions.

Some of those blows, wild though they seemed, caught the deputy here and there. He backed in a flurried move, still very quick on his feet.

"Stand up to me, you dancing monkey," yelled Jingo. His tangled, strawlike tow hair over his eyes. One eye blinking rapidly in the round, almost boyish, clean-shaven face. Grinning though. His opponent grinning back.

They squared up to each other. Fists pumping. Jingo not so eager now, keeping away from the young Mexican man's snakelike arms.

Blood ran from Johnny's lips beneath the thin black moustache, trickled down his chin, stained his shirt-front.

They came together with fists pumping. They were both scoring now. This was elemental, savage, thoughtless even. The crowd screamed and yelled and the dust swirled and thickened till it almost hid the fighters from the gaze of the watchers.

They moved forward into a tighter circle, peering, gesticulating, screaming, almost becoming part of the mêlée it seemed.

The two men staggered like maimed spectres out of the dust and weaved away in opposite directions as if seeking each other and were pushed and jostled and shouted at.

But then there was more shouting of a different kind as two horsemen appeared on the scene and were greeted in different ways.

Apart, Jingo and Johnny turned to face Sheriff Jim Linlatter and another man. A tall man not as fat as Sheriff Jim but of about the same age, and burly. Also with a matched moustache, greying, but as flourishing, grinning as they both reined in.

Jingo and Johnny came together again. The former reached out and grasped his opponent's hand.

"It was a good fight, pizen, an' you

served me good."

"Hell, you had bruises beforehand, *amigo*," said Johnny Tortuga.

"Look at you two," put in Jim Linlatter, "Get yourselves cleaned up for Godsakes."

At the pump round back, Jingo said, between watery splutters, "You know what is the matter with me, ol' pard, why I am as cantankerous as a goddam ol' goat?"

"I hadn't thought about it," said Johnny.

"Since I was a tad I've been in the tail-end of the beef business. Followin' the asses of hundreds of dusty, smelly, stupid damn' cows."

"You're a good cowman."

"Horseshit," said Jingo violently.

"Cool down, son!"

"Sorry. But I've often thought . . . " Jingo let his sentence tail off.

"Thought what?" queried Johnny Tortuga.

"I could do a job like yours," said Jingo. "A deppity. I'd get a helluva lot more satisfaction outa that."

"Sheriff Jim only needs but one deputy I think," said Johnny doubtfully.

"I guess. Oh, well . . . "

* * *

A mite later, back in the office with the returned sheriff and his friend, the Mexican deputy still looked as if he had escaped from wild dogs. He winced as his bruised hand was gripped by the fist of the sheriff's erstwhile saddle-pard, introduced to him as Ed Gallion.

"I heard of you, Mr Gallion," Johnny said.

12

THE cousins got on to the trail of the two men they were after almost by accident, by calling at the outlawish burg that Rimrock and Pinker had visited earlier, and had killed two men there. But had the locals done anything about it? Not in this town, nossir!

Some of 'em had seen those two killers in action. Professional. A gun. A knife. *Uu-uu-ergh!*

But the two cousins weren't fazed by any horrendous tales. Those two bastards had killed their kinfolk. Point us in the right direction they said and some of the townies tried to do this.

"I remember them two from way back," said somebody afterwards. "The one who looks like a walking skelington is called Josh. The other one, him with the wall eyes an' the scraggly beard, is called Mack. They're drifters. Hardcases. If anybody can go up agin Pinker an' Rimrock them two can."

"I'd like to see that," said another individual. "But I ain't about to stick my neck out goin' lookin' for it."

That was their creed. Non-involvement. They forgot about Rimrock and Pinker. Forgot about the two vengeful cousins, Josh and Mack.

But Josh and Mack were good trackers. And the wall-eyed Mack was a good talker. And the silent Josh, whose jib looked like a death's head, scared some folk by his very presence.

And Rimrock and Pinker were sort of moving through legitimate circles, probably trying to find a quiet, legitimate billet were they could light down and lay low. But, in doing so, they couldn't disguise their natures — particularly runty Rimrock with his boiled red visage. And Pinker, not aiming to kill anybody else for a while, was showing off his charm a mile a minute.

Particularly with the ladies.

They wanted someplace with an express office so they could get in touch with their go-between, Callicot. They had other connections but none they completely trusted. They called in on a couple of Pinker's girl-friends, and one of Rimrock's. They served their purpose, broke the dusty monotony of the trail, but no more.

Then they found a little quiet town. A quiet town like Lobo Peaks. Not an important town. Until things happened there in the same way that they had happened in Lobo Peaks, although the boys hadn't actually gone to this second quiet town in order to kill somebody.

They booked a spacious room in a quiet hotel. They had a quiet meal in a local saloon while that was still quiet. They visited a quiet express office presided over by an affable fat gent and they sent off their wire. Then all they had to do was wait.

Rimrock wondered whether there was

a whorehouse in this place. But for once his handsome friend didn't go along with him on this, said whores were too talky and they (the smart boys) couldn't take even the teeniest risk right at the end of the game. The game was played. Now all they had to do was pick up their full winnings. And then look for another game.

"Mebbe Callicot will have somep'n else for us," Pinker added.

"I'm easy," said Rimrock. And he commenced to get good and drunk.

On their way to the place they had stopped off at a small ranch to water their horses, a newish, smallish spread run by a youngish couple with one son, a boy of seven who had taken a shine to Pinker but, as kids sometimes would, had questioned Rimrock about his red face. He had been told off by his ma as she served them coffee and her husband, a weedy nervous-type character, had watched and listened.

His spouse was no fashion-plate but

Pinker had charmed her anyway, just to keep in practice.

At the time Rimrock hadn't thought this was a good idea. All they had wanted, for Chrissakes, was water for the cayuses, and some coffee. And they had purchased a few extra provisions from those people. It just seemed like Pinker, the twinkling fancypants bastard, just could not help himself. But the weedy rancher hadn't looked kindly on his missus, who though resembling a horse, was preenin' and flutterin' for this handsome young stranger's benefit. Not that the gink said anything about that — didn't even make a gesture or utter a misword.

It was him who directed the two strangers to the town. And his missus and son were waving to them until he jerked 'em indoors.

When Josh and Mack, two more ill-assorted characters, turned up at the ranch, the seven-year old kid was intrigued. But his parents, even his mother, were more wary.

They didn't use any hands and, as they were quite a spell away from town, didn't get many visitors. The rancher had told his missus off about what he called her lolly-gagging. It was good job that neither of these other two strangers was good-looking.

They were the reverse of that in fact. A wall-eye in a wispy-bearded jib. And, as for the other one, he had a jib like a skull and walked as if he were about to fall apart.

They were hardhats though. They didn't want any water or coffee or anything. All they wanted were the answers to some questions.

They were somewhat intimidating, these two. But, whether or not, the rancher, still smarting at his wife's treatment of the previous pair of strangers (particularly the fancy one) was quite willing to answer questions. And it seemed like these two jaspers disliked that fancypants as much as the rancher did. And they were almost affable as they left, the cadaverous one even turning in his saddle to wave at the boy.

And that was how cousins Mack and Josh came to that quiet town to meet their destinies. And were more than willing to do so.

★ ★ ★

"We can use him," said Ed Gallion, meaning Jingo. "We can use 'em both, in fact."

"We can't have 'em both," Sheriff Jim Linlatter said. "Somebody has to look after the town. That'll have to be Johnny like before. He's the regular deputy. Anyway, I wouldn't leave that big crazy ranny in charge of anything."

"Yes, mebbe he would be better helpin' us," Gallion conceded. "As he seems so anxious to do this."

"Rafe Renvane was Jingo's friend too. Everybody liked ol' Rafe."

"I remember Rafe. He was a good man. And a good Ranger in his day . . . Well, as long as you don't object to usin' Jingo . . . "

"No, it ain't that, Ed. He'll be a posse-member. But I can't make him a town deputy. The city fathers wouldn't sit still for that. Jingo ramrodding Lobo Peaks while the real law was off a-trailing! Nossir. Y' see what I mean, Ed?"

"Yes, I see, Jim."

"But I ain't saying that Jingo wouldn't be able to handle himself on the trail. He certainly would. And there are other volunteers."

"We won't need any more, Jim."

"Just as you say. So now I have to tell Johnny he's staying and Jingo is coming with us. Johnny ain't gonna like that. Though them two was fightin' like cat an' dog when you first saw 'em, they have actually been friends since they were sprigs, an' sort of sparring partners too. Still an' all . . . " Jim Linlatter's voice tailed off.

Ed Gallion said, "But like you've already admitted, Jim, Johnny is your deputy and the town's man. I'll back you on that."

"Mebbe you'll have to. Here's Johnny now."

They were walking side by side. Jingo and Johnny. They were clean and armed and they didn't look too damaged. They walked straight and both with a bit of a swagger and an air of enthusiasm.

Linlatter and Gallion were seated on a rocking chair apiece on the stoop outside the Lariat stores. There were three such chairs there for the use of customers or anybody who happened along. It was a good place for a chinwag. Sitting in the sun. Smoking, dozing, or desultory gabbing.

Until a few minutes ago the third chair had been occupied by old Simon the storekeeper. But he was inside now, tending a customer.

After the fight, the appearance of the sheriff and his friend, Gallion, the town had gone pretty quiet.

Now, when Jingo and his sparring

partner Johnny were only a few yards away from the two older men, there were noises from the direction of the saloon, Digger's Place.

Somebody seemed to be breaking furniture. And there were shouting voices.

"What the hell!" exclaimed Linlatter and he heaved up his bulk from the gently rocking chair.

Gallion followed suit and they both turned. They marched side by side towards the saloon. Jingo and Johnny brought up the rear. To the boys the somewhat elderly gents moved with admirable alacrity. The younkers hastened to catch them. But it was still the sheriff who butted through the batwings first. And Gallion was to the side of his friend as they spread out, two wily old hounds acting as one.

It was a bunch of Jingo's ranchhand pards who were causing the trouble. They were hazing the old swamper, a bleary-eyed ex-miner called Roamer, whose long life mainly under the hot sun had caused him to be kind of puddled. He was whirling his heavy broom around his head and cursing obscenely at the four rannies who danced in front of him.

Things it seemed had hotted up quickly. Sprawled chairs, two with legs missing, and one overturned table told their story.

The ranchhands had plied the oldster with booze before beginning to goad him. Roamer wasn't naturally pugnacious. But he had been under strict orders not to drink because of the peculiar things the hooch did to his nature.

There had been a good fight. But the ranchhands' champion, Jingo, had not won. Nobody had won. The boys had been expecting their big feller to lay that fancy Mexican deputy in the dust. It was their contention that he had been prevented from doing so by the arrival of the deputy's boss and that other older jasper whom none of them had seen before.

The fact that the two contestants seemed to have finished up like bosom friends cut no ice with the disgruntled rannies. Their fun had been cut short prematurely. They wanted some more.

Now they were getting some all right. By the time the law entered Digger's Place some of the townsfolk were taking a hand, pushing in front of the irate Roamer, protecting him while having to dodge his whirling broom at the same time.

A townsman was knocked sprawling by a roundhouse swing from a cowboy. Jim Linlatter was on top of things by then and he grabbed the cowboy by the shoulder and yelled, "Hold up there, all o' you."

Things got frenetic then. Jumbled sort of. Almost funny. But then not quite so funny.

The offended cowboy didn't know who had grabbed him. He just automatically wrenched his shoulder free and whirled, swung a fist. It wasn't necessarily a well-placed blow, just a lucky one. It caught the sheriff on the angle of the jaw.

The ranny's swinging momentum had given his blow power. Linlatter, caught by surprise, was knocked backwards.

The big lawman, who carried more than a mite too much weight, lost balance entirely and, twisting with painful awkwardness, fell across the overturned table which had been earlier tumbled.

The ensuing crash was as loud as any that had been heard before. The advancing Gallion almost tripped over his friend's bulk as the big lawman tried to extricate himself from the now broken table. But Gallion had his gun out then. And he righted himself.

He was not a man for shouting it seemed. He pistol-whipped the offending ranny across the side of the head and laid him unconscious on the boards.

It was Jingo who did the shouting now, facing his ranchhand pards.

"What in the hell is the matter with you? It's over now. It's over!"

They looked sheepish. One of them still supine on the floor, not even groaning.

Gallion and Johnny were trying to help the sheriff to his feet. He yelped with pain. Then in the almost-quietness his words were plain. "Goddamit, I think my arm is busted!"

13

"THEM two over there," said Rimrock with a slight sideways jerk of his head. "They've bin watchin' us ever since we came in."

"Which two?" queried Pinker, beginning to turn in his seat.

"Don't look round, Goddamit. The one with the wall eye is lookin' right at us now. Didn't you spot 'em earlier?"

"Oh, I spotted 'em all right. But I ain't got such a good view as you have, have I?"

"I guess not. Stay easy. They're pretendin' they ain't lookin' now, both of 'em."

"Mebbe the one with the funny eye allus stares at folk like that," said Pinker.

"The one who looks like a skeleton was staring as well."

"Mebbe they think they know us

from some place. But I wouldn't think they're law, would you?"

"Nope. And I'm sure I ain't seen either of 'em before. I'd remember 'em if I had."

"Me too, I guess. But I'll take a better look at 'em when I have a chance."

The two subjects of their conversation — although Pinker and Rimrock didn't know this of course — were having a similar discussion.

Cadaverous Josh, usually taciturn, was saying for the second time, "It must be them. Description fits prime."

"Yeh," said Mack, usually the talky one. But he didn't sound completely convinced. It was as if, after the long trail, he was tired of the searching and didn't care as much as he had appeared to do in the first place.

He was the gabby one, the nervous one. Josh, seemingly indolent, a man who looked as if he were dying on his feet, was the action-packed killer.

"I'm gonna find out," he said.

"I oughta do that," said Mack.

Josh, butt already off his seat, looked at his cousin. "You'd talk too much," he said. And that was a fact. And Mack knew it.

They were sitting near the door. Their quarry, the two men they now knew to be called Pinker and Rimrock, were in a corner not far from the long bar in the still quiet saloon in this quiet town.

"Watch me," Josh went on. "I'll draw them out."

"You want me to stay here then?"

"Yes. It might look too sort of obvious if we both go over there."

Mack didn't quite get his partner's drift. But he went along with it like he usually did.

Josh got right out of his chair and turned his bony body around, his movements spare and calculated but not too quick. He was as cold as a zombie and sometimes he actually looked like one.

Mack watched him make his lanky

way across the floor. He seemed hesitant and ungainly. Anybody would've thought that. But Mack didn't. They had been tads together. Mack had seen Josh kill his first man. Long before he himself had killed his first one.

But there were two of them over there in the corner of the barroom, and Mack didn't try to kid himself that those two were not professionals. He was still a mite bemused, not sure whether Josh and he were doing this the right way or not.

★ ★ ★

The big rawboned medico was of the same generation as Linlatter and Gallion. His name was Beedle and he was noted for his outspokenness, bordering on insult, particularly with argumentative patients. And he was dealing with one right now.

"You ain't about to ride any place," he said. "That's a mighty nasty fracture you collected for yourself and you ain't a young sprig o' sixteen any more full o' piss an' vinegar."

"You can strap it up, can't you, Doc?" said Jim Linlatter. "Hell, I've got to lead a posse. I . . . "

"Hoss-shit!" Beedle had a deep, thunderous voice and, when he needed to, he used it with great advantage. Folks in the street outside the law office could probably hear it now. As he went on, "You want to crock that arm for good, you goddam jackass? You want to finish up as an old cripple? Fat chance you'd have then against some fast young gunny, huh? Huh?"

It was a question that didn't need an answer and the sheriff was momentarily bereft of speech. Like he usually did when he was uncertain he nervously stroked his luxuriant moustache while the doc, half-grinning now, and the others watched him. Deputy Johnny, big tow-headed Jingo, erect, moustached Ed Gallion. It was the latter who spoke and his was a voice that carried authority.

117

"Doctor Beedle is right, Jim. There ain't two ways about it, is there?"

Another question. And the sheriff had to answer this one. Shrugged, nodded, began, "I guess . . . " Let his voice tail off.

"Give me a badge an' I'll lead the posse," went on Gallion. "I'll take Johnny an' Jingo. They're all I'll need. You stay an' mind the shop."

The last sentence was an unfortunate turn of phrasing. Gallion had always been an outspoken and not always tactful man.

"I ain't no damn' invalid," exploded Linlatter.

"No, just a damn' idiot," said the rawboned medico. And then Jim Linlatter could only sort of splutter beneath his moustache. But the others had won the day and he had to give in. He had made his show. He had had to do that. But he was a philosophical cuss. His arm in a sling, he lumbered to his feet.

"I've got badges," he snorted.

118

"I'll get 'em, Sheriff Jim," said Deputy Johnny.

His chief gave him a look fit to frizzle him and he stayed where he was.

Unfortunately, it was Linlatter's good right arm that was busted. But he handed out tin stars with his left hand, without comment but with a certain aggression, both Gallion and Jingo thanking him with the utmost politeness.

Big tow-head Jingo said, "My boss'll have to know."

"I'll see that that is taken care of," snapped the sheriff. "A boy can do that."

"Some of the hands are still around."

"I hope they ain't about to start acting up again," said Linlatter darkly.

"They ain't," said Jingo. "I've told 'em an' they'll stay told. They'll hafta be going back soon. A couple volunteered . . . "

"We don't need 'em," cut in the new leader of the posse.

"Just as you say, Mr Gallion," said

Jingo with an almost gentleness.

"Let's get set then."

★ ★ ★

Rimrock said, "That queer skeleton-man is on his way over."

"It takes all sorts as they say," commented Pinker. He sounded languid. "I ain't about to turn an' greet him. Keep an eye on him, friend."

"I'm doing that, ain't I?" snorted Rimrock.

Goddam fancy play-acting bastard!

It was the skeleton-man's gun that Pinker saw first. He had seen Rimrock's eyes widen in his sore-looking, *sour-looking* red face but had merely taken it for some kind of umbrage. Rimrock seemed plumb full of umbrage lately.

But the gun was pointing at Rimrock. And then it was sort of pointing at both of them. And the gangly man with the skull-face had his back to the rest of the folk in the barroom — Pinker and his pard being in a corner an' all — and doubtless his friend by the door had his eyes on them anyway.

Skull-face had the gun almost tucked into his belly, the butt of the gun that is, almost hidden, though he had no belly to speak of really. But the barrel was pointing straight and was as steady and certain as the death that came to all species sooner or later. And Rimrock and Pinker didn't aim to make it sooner.

Rimrock had seen the man draw. Just before the man got to the table. He *thought* he had seen the man draw — but he hadn't: you didn't always see a snake's tongue, the snap of the jaws of a desert gila.

"Hands on the top o' the table, both o' you," the man said.

"What in hell do you want?" said Rimrock, moving his empty hands up.

"You two killed my aunt an' uncle," said the man.

It hit home. They had killed a few lately. There had been a sod-buster. And his missus who'd taken a hand.

Pinker had knifed her.

Maybe Rimrock's sun-bleached eyes in the ravaged red face gave him away.

And the eyes in the skull-face of the tall man opposite were looking hard at Rimrock. Pinker came up with his blade which had been resting on his knee beneath the table as the cadaverous interloper had approached him and Rimrock.

The gaunt man's gun went off. But by that time he had been ripped from brisket to breast. Powerful, slicing, cutting deeper all the time. Spilling his intestines and reaching upwards and penetrating his heart. A butcher's work.

He screamed, falling forward across the table. And there was more than one scream as Rimrock fell back in his chair clutching his ear — or what was left after the tall man's bullet had gone through it, tearing it away, the bloody slug smashing into the wall behind.

Rimrock hit the wall too. Then he

fell of his chair sideways. The gaunt man slipped off the table and joined Rimrock on the floor amid a welter of broken glass, spilled whisky and blood. Rimrock sobbing, clutching his head, blood running thickly down the side of his face.

The skull-face grinned at Rimrock. The skullface didn't say anything.

Rimrock struggled upwards, drew his gun with his right hand, his left hand still clutching his wound. There seemed to be blood everywhere.

Pinker had thrown his bloodied knife downwards. The blade was embedded in a floorboard and seemed to be quivering. Rising, turning, Pinker had his gun in his fist now.

The man by the window had his gun out. Folks scattered out of the line of fire. But the shot from the man at the window almost pinked a fat gink who hadn't been quick enough. The bullet missed the men in the corner; the wounded one, the dead one, the standing one with the levelled gun.

The man by the door whipped through the batwings and was out of sight.

Pinker went after him.

Rimrock screamed something, wild, inarticulate. Gun in hand, he went after his partner. He lurched from side to side, spattering drops of bright blood all around.

When he caught up with his killer-pard, Pinker was standing on the sidewalk, gun in hand, looking about him.

"He moved like a streak. I didn't even see which way he went."

There weren't many people in the street.

"My ear," whined Rimrock. "*My ear!*"

14

IN the past Sheriff Jim had briefly mentioned to his deputy, his friend in the Texas Rangers, the man named Ed Gallion, a captain and the finest officer Jim Linlatter had ever served under. Like Jim, Ed had long since left the Rangers but, Jim said, last time he had heard of Gallion some folks were still calling him 'Cap'n'.

Johnny started to call the big man 'Cap'n'. The latter made no comment about this, merely smiled thinly beneath his moustache. Johnny reflected that Sheriff Jim and the Cap'n were much alike. He gave the Cap'n the same respect that he gave the sheriff. And the third member of the trio did the same. Jingo the smiling deputy.

But they were three professionals who had a job to do, a mission to fulfil. They did not smile much.

Although Gallion hadn't said so, he seemed to know where he was going. The other two had to assume, as they would, that the older man knew far more about the lawless lands than they did. They bivouacked by night and rode by day. They had brought plenty of supplies, and doubtless Gallion knew where they could get more if they needed them.

★ ★ ★

The consensus was that it had been pure self-defence. The cadaverous man had drawn his gun first. He would've probably shot the red-faced man dead if the red-faced man's pard hadn't taken a hand and slit the aggressor's gullet. That had been too swift to watch. A neat job, if messy. But the initial gun-pulling had been noticed by transfixed onlookers.

Then the dead man's pard, over there by the door, had started shooting, before lighting out like a cat with tail on fire.

126

The two strangers (hell, weren't they all strangers?) hadn't caught up with the running man, a wall-eyed ugly. Somebody said later that they thought they had seen him riding out of town.

Pinker and Rimrock would have gone after him. But they had to wait in town for their man Callicot to turn up with some more *dinero*. And besides, there was Rimrock and his ear. Or his lack of ear: just a fragment of bloody gristle now with a hole in it.

They were both at the local doc's surgery when the local sheriff paid them a visit. He was big and slow-moving and affable and no trouble at all. Yeh, it had been self-defence all right, there was no mistake about that. Did either of the two gents know the dead man and his missing pard? No, they said, and now they were telling the truth. Crazy people they said.

They figured they knew what it had been about: those two had been on a vengeance trail. But the red-faced one-eared man and his fancy-talking young partner didn't tell the sheriff this.

They figured they had to catch up with the other one sooner or later — before he got reinforcements or something.

They waited impatiently for Callicot, and Pinker was as fidgety as a young grizzly with a burr in his ass. And Rimrock, a bandage tied over his head and down under his chin, holding a pad on his wound, was cloudy-eyed with pain. He lay on a bed in their hotel room and tried to rest, cussing from time to time as Pinker paced around him.

They had seen the doc, the law, other assorted town-bods. They had even seen the undertaker, who had wanted to know who was going to pay for the burial of the gutted cadaver. For some obscure reason he seemed to think that Pinker and Rimrock were going to volunteer. But of course they turned him down flat and Rimrock said that as the jasper had been like a skeleton anyway why not just dig a hole and throw him into it?

The undertaker hadn't been amused. He looked a bit like a skeleton himself. He left in a huff. Pinker laughed in his nasty humourless way. Rimrock, who had made the joke, tried to laugh too, but he wound up almost crying.

"F'r Chrissakes, hoss, sit down," he said now.

Pinker plumped on to a wooden chair by the window. "If that skunk Callicot is aiming to double-cross us I'll find him an' I'll have his tripes," he said.

The one-eared bandage-festooned Rimrock didn't hear him, had he done so might have said that Callicot couldn't afford to play that way.

But, almost as if he had been reading his partner's mind, Rimrock at length did say, "The doc said I should rest up, not ride, or this ear might turn mighty nasty."

"What are you?" demanded Pinker. "A goddam wiltin' lily?"

There was no reply to that. And Rimrock was at last dozing off.

Mack figured that Josh was stone dead. Carved like a pig. There was nothing he had been able to do about it, he told himself. He hadn't thought it had been a good idea, Josh approaching those two killers on his own, Mack remembered, told himself now. But Josh had taken no notice and Mack had gone along with Josh's idea as usual.

They would've killed me too had I stood up to 'em, thought Mack, I had to get away then. I'll fix them two later, by Gar I will! But right now he felt kind of lost without cousin Josh.

He rode hard. His horse had the bit between his teeth: he seemed to be running away from something also. Mack didn't even know were they were going. He let the beast carry him an' that was that.

The night was dark when he finally halted the beast. He hunkered down, looking back at the way he had come.

There was only a sliver of moon and the stars were like bright pinpricks in the heavens. He couldn't see anything of course and all he heard was the soft soughing of a cooling breeze.

Really, it was a pretty good night, but Mack didn't appreciate that. He didn't know whether to bivouac, to mount up again and ride on, or to find a hole and climb down into it and maybe pull it in over him.

But he remained where he was while his horse browsed contentedly.

Maybe those two bastards would come upon him and he could bushwhack 'em, a thought which got away from him. He let himself slide into a reclining position, and then he must have dropped off.

Something must have wakened him. He didn't know how long he'd been asleep but the night was still with him, still the same. But it wasn't so quiet. He recognized the sound of hoofbeats but was a bit puzzled because they were coming from the opposite direction than the way he would have expected. He rose, trying to gather his wits together.

Thinking he was needed, the horse ambled forward. "Easy, boy," hissed Mack. "Quiet."

He remembered that as he rode in the beginning of the night he had spotted ranch buildings in the distance and then had heard a bit later the lowing of cattle, though he hadn't seen any. He hadn't seen or heard anything after that except the wide undulating plains with no real hills, and the skies; and he had heard the breeze.

The hoofbeats got louder. Not a lot of riders. Two or three maybe. Two? But it couldn't be that pair of killers, could it, not coming from that direction? Maybe it was night riders from that ranch. Or rannies on their way back after a night on the town.

He stood by his horse and drew his hand-gun and held it down by his side and faced the way of the rapidly growing noise, the hammer of hoofbeats. And he waited.

★ ★ ★

Doc Beedle hadn't told him he had to take to his bed. Had the outspoken medico done so he would've been sent away with a sizeable bug in his ear. Jim Linlatter and he were two of a kind, chivvied each other, respected each other, insulted each other.

So I can't ride, Jim thought, so be it. But I'm still sheriff at this hootin' town and up to a point I'll do as I please. I'll go to the livery and borrow a gig and a trotter (I can handle reins with one hand for Pete's sake) and I'll go for a spin.

Because of his arm he had had an uncomfortable night. But he was still restless; early. He knew, however, that the old hostler was an early riser too, most probably would be open for business.

This proved to be the case and only a

short while after his coffee and biscuits Linlatter was out on the plains with the sun in his eyes — not too hot yet — and the breezes in his face. He figured that, after a fine spin, he would have an appetite for one of the big breakfasts he regaled himself with from time to time, despite the fact that pesky Beedle had told him over and over that he ought to cut down on his weight.

He was approaching a draw with fringes of mesquite skirting it when he heard the shooting.

Then the shooting stopped and he figured the shooter must have heard his wheels. He stopped the horse, halted the gig. He was in a pretty vulnerable position. He peered and he listened.

In the dip a man appeared, walked towards him. He had a gun in each hand but the hands hung loosely at his side. Linlatter saw the figure and the guns with the sun glinting on them but he didn't see much else because of the sun.

He raised the hand on his good arm above him in a half-sign of peace and he kept the hand above his eyes, shading them. But, when the figure called, "That you, Jim?" he lowered the hand again.

"That you, Gunfighter?" he mocked.

"It is."

"I might've known!" Jim Linlatter climbed carefully down from his perch.

"What happened to you? You been in a fight?"

"Sort of." Linlatter approached the tall old man who turned about and they walked side by side down the slope.

How old must he be? Eighty? More? Folks who had known him in the old, old days must have thought of him as long since gone to his Maker. He had been old when he first appeared in Lobo Peaks, but not for a long stay. He was a man who came and went. He had been doing that ever since.

Then, at first, his rep had come before him. And his name, which Jim

Linlatter had to dredge up from his memory now.

Sid Mallow, ex-marshal, killer, bounty-hunter, troubleshooter, the master of all kinds of weapon. But Sheriff Linlatter had never known Sid Mallow to use a weapon on the streets of Lobo Peaks. The notorious killer had seemed a gentle man and had been no trouble at all.

Linlatter had used him for a jailer for a time. Nobody messed with him; not him. He didn't seem to mind his lowly position in the community, a watcher over drunks and fractious cowboys. But not for long. Again he went on his way.

The only thing about him that was consistent was the fact that he kept practising. He was a connoisseur of weapons, particularly handguns — and he kept practising.

Sheriff Linlatter reflected now that when he said "I might've known," yes, he should've done. This draw was one of the old man's practising

136

places, maybe his main one. And, like the others, away from habitation and livestock. As always, no trouble to anything, man nor beast.

Sid Mallow. In his early days in Lobo Peaks, he hadn't seemed keen to answer to that name any more. Nobody knew whether it was his right one or not anyway. A few folk who considered they were friends of his called him Sid. Others called him Mr Mallow. But somehow that didn't seem to fit their image of a killing gunfighter.

He came and went and, although he didn't show it much, he obviously got older. And folks began to refer to him as The Old Gunfighter.

"I didn't know you were back," Linlatter said.

"You must be slippin', Jim," the old man said. "Or your informants ain't what they used to be. Did you hit your head when you fell over an busted your arm?"

"I might've done," said Linlatter.

Seemed like The Old Gunfighter

might have his sources of information too.

When he had worked in the jailhouse he had always seemed to keep his finger on the pulse of things.

He was stooped a little because he was tall. But apart from that he didn't seem any older than the first time Linlatter had seen him, riding down the main drag of Lobo Peaks on a dusty horse.

Even then he had worn steel-rimmed spectacles, seemed to be wearing the same pair right now. Maybe it was his eyes that had determined him to give up gunslinging for a living. But it was amazing how keen those blue eyes seemed behind the lenses of those mundane glasses and how unwrinkled the area was around there in the lean weatherbeaten face.

He had his targets, bottles and cans and sticks, on rocks of different sizes and elevations and he had his guns, his old stand-bys, a matched pair of bone-handled Navy Colts. Linlatter wondered where the old man had his other gear stashed. He could be staying any place. But it wasn't in town or the sheriff would have known about that.

"You still shoot good?" the old man asked.

"Middlin'."

"Don't try an' snow me, bucko. Can you shoot with your arm in a sling? As I remember, you used to be able to shoot with both hands just like me."

"Yeh." Linlatter made a cross-arm draw, pulling his Colt with his left hand. He fired rapidly. Three shots. Two bottles shattered to gleaming smithereens. The third bullet pinged off a rock and ricocheted away.

"Drat it," said the sheriff.

"Not bad," said The Old Gunfighter. "A mite hasty on that last one. But not bad at all."

15

THEY met the man on the trail in the early morning and Johnny Tortuga recognized him immediately. He was easy to remember. That wall eye and that ridiculous wispy beard. One of the two hardcases who had called in at Lobo Peaks on a vengeance trail. But where was his partner?

He told them where his partner was, though he couldn't know if his partner was still above the sod. Seemed like he — his name was Mack he said — had been riding a long while. It was time to turn back now though, he said, and he'd be purely gratified if the three gents would let him ride along with them.

He'd show 'em where those two killers were at, he said. If they were still there. He hoped so. They didn't seem to have followed him. But, if they had, maybe they'd be come upon on the trail. He'd purely enjoy a necktie party with those two as the guests of honour.

He certainly was a talky one!

"Come along if you like," said Ed Gallion, curtly.

And Johnny Tortuga jerked a thumb in the direction of the tall, moustached, elder man who had just spoken and added, "And if you do come along you also do what the Cap'n says, y'understand, *amigo*?"

Mack looked from one to the other of them, lastly at the big tow-headed rough-looking younker who hadn't spoken, and said, "Sure I understand. Sure. Me an' Josh was pards for a long time and that fancypants skunk carved him like he was pig meat. The other one got wounded so mebbe they're still hanging around. I want their hides."

"You'll have 'em my way," said Gallion.

He had the last word, and the talky

Mack was silent then, ranging up, riding side by side with them.

Mack had ridden a hell of a lot further than he thought. He had run as if the hounds of hell were on his heels. He tried not to admit this. But he was going back, wasn't he? He was even impatient.

It seemed that the big man they called Cap'n knew the place, had an idea how far it was. They didn't want to hit it in the night though, he said, that might be a giveaway. And he didn't aim to have either horses or men getting overtired. They would bivouac. They would hit the town come morning.

He had a great air of authority and was obviously a seasoned campaigner at this sort of thing. Mack didn't try and argue with him.

As things turned out, they couldn't have got there in time for anything anyway.

They learned that the two men they sought had left yesterday while there was still light and after another man had turned up and sort of collected them. A fat little man who didn't seem to be a very good rider.

A barman said he had heard the three talking and the little man had wanted to stay overnight and rest but the other two had roughshod him, had ridden him out in fact.

"But there was somep'n about hopping a train," the barman added.

"Where's the nearest junction?" Gallion asked and the barman told him. And they learned that the trio had gone in that direction. If Gallion had any idea of who the little fat stranger was he didn't then divulge the fact. It was a balmy morning by then. They went on their way.

★ ★ ★

Somebody else they knew had thought about hopping a train. Somebody that three of them knew anyway. Sheriff Jim Linlatter.

The sheriff had been doing a lot of thinking, particularly after meeting The Old Gunfighter and persuading that worthy to come back to Lobo Peaks for a drink.

The old man was greeted with great affability but with no great surprise, except maybe "you're here again then, are you?" or words to that effect. He twinkled at everybody from behind his steel-rimmed specs and smiled his gentle smile.

For the most part the two old friends and colleagues were left alone to imbibe and talk. Desultory at first. And then Linlatter said, "Sid, do you remember when you were jailer for me for a time?"

"Of course I remember. I ain't in my dotage yet."

"Could you do it again?"

"If I had to I guess. Why?"

Linlatter told him why. Told him the whole story, but as briefly as possible. And, when the sheriff had finished, The Old Gunfighter asked, "Won't

Doc Beedle object?"

"If he does it'll cut no ice with me this time. I'll take the gig an' I'll leave it at the way station . . . First of all, though, I've got to go to the ranch where young Jingo works and tell his boss that Jingo is working for me. Jingo's pards will already have taken the news there, but it's my duty to go and explain things better I guess and besides, Jingo's boss, Cy O'Day, is a friend o' mine."

"I know Cy. I ain't seen him yet this time, but I'm camping in one of his line huts on the north range. The one that ain't used much 'cos the cattle doesn't like the wind up there. Cy said I could use it any time."

"Cy's a good man."

"I could tell Cy . . . "

"I want you here, old-timer . . . Anyway, if the doc wants to know where I am that's where I'll be gone, to the ranch. He ain't to know I'm going on to the railhead."

"You ain't told me where the train

is gonna take you."

"A longish way. To the borderlands. The Mexican end. It's a complicated story so I won't bore you with it. It ain't really straight in my own mind yet. It's just something I've got to find out . . . "

"To do with the killing of Rafe Renvane?"

"That and others."

"You know what you're doing I guess."

"I wouldn't say that, not all the way. But I hope so."

"Mebbe I ought to come with you."

"Like I said," — the sheriff sounded a mite exasperated now — "I want you here."

"I ain't yet agreed to stay here."

"Will you?"

"All right, I will."

"Till I get back?"

"Till you get back," said The Old Gunfighter. He added darkly, "If you get back."

"If I don't, mebbe they'll make you

sheriff of Lobo Peaks."

"That'll be the day."

"Hell, you ain't no common jailer, you'll be more or less holding down a lawman's job while me an' the other boys are missing. Nobody's gonna go against you and you know it."

"Do I? Well, all right. When do you aim to go?"

"Any time now. As soon as I've seen the hostler to tell him that his boy can pick up the gig at the way station if they want it. I've got to go to Cy's place first of course."

"How will you get back? Back after the end of it I mean."

The end of it! That was an ominous phrase. But — "I'll think o' somep'n," Sheriff Linlatter said.

And he rose to his feet.

★ ★ ★

"I couldn't carry all that *dinero* with me," Callicot said. "And, anyway, I had to make sure everything was done.

It has all been done, hasn't it?"

"Godamighty!" exploded Rimrock and was about to go on, when Pinker said almost mildly, "Of course it's all been done. The telegraph told you that in the very words you told me to use. You trust us. You know our rep."

"Yes, yes," said the little fat man hastily, not fooled by the handsome young killer's seeming tractability.

Callicot was sweating profusely in his expensive but rather too heavy riding gear. He wasn't at all happy. "It's a pity about that other killing," he said.

"That was unavoidable," said Pinker.

"Hell, we told you," said Rimrock.

"We were forced into it," said Pinker. "Everybody said so. You heard it."

"There's that other man."

"He's to hell an' gone. Anyway, you don't have to worry about him, do you? You get us the rest of our *dinero* an' you can kiss us *adios*."

"I don't know why we have to go through all this goddam toin' an' froin' an' pushin' an' pullin'," said Rimrock.

As usual he wasn't being very articulate but the other two got his drift. Pinker for one could have told him one reason for all the toin' an' froin' etcetera. He knew Callicot's mind, for it was very like his own; devious, tortuous even, slanted towards intrigue for the sake of intrigue. And somewhat unpredictable. Rimrock wouldn't understand that at all.

And probably the person who had hired Callicot to arrange for the four executions (and that was what they had been) to be done had a mind that worked much in the same way as Pinker's and Callicot's did. Somebody who wanted more than anything to cover their tracks as, in his devious way, Callicot was doing now. He was a go-between and nothing more.

Or was he something more, the fat, oily little bastard? Had he — or his principal, or both of them — got some sort of double-cross planned?

You killed the men who killed the men and your tracks were covered completely. And you saved all that *dinero* to boot.

Godamighty, was that it? *Was it?*

But how? Who could do it? Who could take him and Rimrock? Certainly not Callicot. That was laughable.

"The train will be just ahead," Callicot said.

But they could see nothing yet.

Rimrock began to whine about his ear again. Blood was beginning to seep through the bandages.

16

DOC BEEDLE turned up at the law office and discovered that Jim Linlatter had gone again. The good doctor knew that some while ago Jim had returned from a spin in the gig he had hired from the livery stables. Beedle had called to advise the sheriff that he shouldn't go lolly-gagging around too much, thus putting strain on his busted arm, not unless he aimed to lose the prime facility of that once-prime right fin, his favoured one.

Knowing that Linlatter had returned accompanied by The Old Gunfighter, the doc had not been surprised to find that bespectacled character in the office.

But no Sheriff Jim Linlatter.

The Old Gunfighter couldn't — or wouldn't — tell the disgruntled medico much. Knowing the old man from way

151

back, Beedle didn't try too hard. Might as well question the rocks or the wind! The doctor liked The Old Gunfighter. Most townsfolk did. One thing, it looked as if the old man aimed to stay for a while, and that was unusual for him.

He was laying out his gear, taking the pieces one by one from the crumpled expanse of a large and dusty tarp, and placing them gently on the top of the wide, battered desk which he had evidently cleared for that purpose.

There was a considerable armoury. Apart from The Old Gunfighter's old-stage Navy Colts, there were two other handguns which the oldster was maybe keeping for some special purpose. He would use them for practice, that was for sure. He was a collector of weapons. He handled them now with loving care, his lean, still-supple fingers deft but gentle. As if the deadly-looking things were priceless antiques or delicate, finely crafted ornaments. Finely crafted they were and as finely honed and balanced as surgeons' instruments — but, like those, they were tools. But they were not tools of life, they were tools of death and, as Doc Beedle watched the old man tendering them, he felt a strange chill.

Those long, prehensile, seemingly gentle fingers had, in the past, used those tools coldly and with great expertise, used them for the purpose for which they were intended, had used them as a great surgeon used his instruments, but for a grotesquely different and deadly purpose.

Doc Beedle, born and brought up in the West, trained there, cutting his teeth during the war between the States on wounds from revolvers, rifles, carbines, bayonets and various kinds of other cutting weapons, and the tearing, horrendous damage caused by minie balls and exploding shells, knew weapons well — oh, yes — and had a clinical interest in them. He could also use, with fair expertise, a handgun or a rifle. He had once killed, with a knife, a union soldier who had tried to bayonet him from behind, had sliced his ribs and had intended to try again for keeps, had been stabbed in the chest and had died instantly. It was something that still haunted the doctor from time to time, something he would never forget.

The Old Gunfighter's two back-up guns, if they could be called that, were fine examples of the art of making death-dealing tools. Even Doc Beedle had to admit this. God help him, he *knew* guns also.

A beautifully crafted Smith and Wesson .44 calibre pistol with a short barrel and a yellow bone grip chased in silver, an easily handled, specially made belly gun that could be hidden inside a man's shirt or tucked in his pants and still be drawn quickly without any trouble at all. And, beside it, dwarfing it, a long-barrelled Colt Dragoon which, though also a .44 had, all in all, been made to a much larger specification. Some professionals liked the Dragoon for its weight and its power, the long barrel which they figured gave greater accuracy.

This latter six-shooter looked as if it had just come out of the factory, but Doc Beedle knew that this couldn't be the case. The Dragoon was a pretty old gun now, had been superseded by lighter Colts, even the Navy one, or the ubiquitous Peacemaker. And there were others by S & W and Remington of course.

Maybe this Dragoon had been specially built, or specially modified at least. The doctor wondered where the old gunslinger had procured it, but he didn't ask. It had a walnut butt which shone like it had been varnished and a hammer on it that had a large round thumb-grip, something that the doc hadn't seen before, thinking that this feature was kind of clumsy-looking, making the miniature cannon-like aspect of the gun more marked than was usual.

155

ATCHISON LIBRARY
401 KANSAS
ATCHISON, KS 66002

The Old Gunfighter had no less than a third back-up weapon, which he now produced from the folds of the tarp, making his full quota of handguns up to five. The fifth was a real belly gun. Almost as small as a derringer but obviously carrying more than one or two shots, the circular cartridge section gleaming in the centre of the small strangely tubby-looking body. Gender indeterminate, an ugly weapon with a cut-down stub of a trigger, a filed-down sight, a barrel that looked like a man's thumb and a hammer that seemed to be folded back on a sort of swivel . . . Suddenly the doc had had his fill of weapons, the sight of them . . . the Winchester leaning against the edge of the desk; the sawn-off shotgun with the sawn-down butt, and the huge Bowie knife that the oldster was now taking out of the tarp, running his thumb gently down the keen, gleaming edge of the wicked broad blade.

And, if you turned, there were the long guns in the rack against the wall — the posse hadn't taken them all, only their own favourites maybe — and the handguns in their chains and their padlock (who had the key now, Sheriff Linlatter or his new deputy, Sid Mallow, The Old Gunfighter?) and the sabre that Jim Linlatter had once taken from a drunken half-crazy ex-soldier-cum-miner — before running him out of town — and kept as a souvenir . . .

"I'll see you later, Sid," said Doc Beedle and he left the office.

"Sure, Doc." The Old Gunfighter's preoccupied reply floated after him.

★ ★ ★

Ed Gallion had agreed to stop for the funeral, of the cousin called Josh that is, so cousin Mack could pay his last respects to the pard he had had since he was a little tad. Mack wasn't short of *dinero*. He paid for the function and the buryers and the folk did old Josh proud, after the undertaker had

157

sewn him up and made him halfway presentable, placed in a long coffin and consigned to the earth while the local preacher, a cadaverous man in appearance not unlike the person he was burying, intoned the words with doleful experience.

Johnny and Jingo took off their hats and tried not to fidget and Gallion was as grave as a churchwarden. Then the folks went down into town for the usual after-burying carousing. But Gallion wouldn't stay for that, and he was adamant now and the boys were glad to go along with him, Mack wiping his eyes, complaining that the dust in the wind had gotten into them up on that Goddam Boot Hill.

★ ★ ★

When Pinker and Rimrock followed Callicot into the smallish town they realized that it was a new one, as smart as pins. They didn't ask its name. They had seen all sorts. This was better than most. This was where, Callicot said, they were to pick up the money. Then maybe they'd stay awhile and maybe they wouldn't. Neither of the two killers seemed to have an opinion about this and their little fat companion was for the most part silent now.

They went to the bank and it was new and square, built of red brick and very substantial-looking. Callicot said there was no need for one of the boys to go in with him but Pinker went anyway, a smiling gentlemanly boy.

In a hotel room they divvied up. Then Callicot said he would be on his way, he'd had enough of horseback riding. A stage halted there. He had checked and there was another one to go today. He would catch it, trail his horse behind. The boys could stop here for a while, he said, if that was what they wanted.

Pinker said maybe they would. Rimrock said nothing. The side of his face was swollen and, a little while ago, he had said that through the bloody swollen stump that had once been his ear, there were stabbing pains. He said he couldn't see straight, couldn't think, that he needed a doctor badly.

But right now the handsome boy seemed more preoccupied with Callicot, even though they had got their full money, him and his pardner, and everything in the garden now seemed rosy except for said pardner's bad ear.

Pinker thought that Callicot had been far too devious — even for Pinker! Rimrock hadn't thought it mattered. Pinker seemed to think that Callicot was involved in some kind of double-cross. They had the *dinero* now. And it was a hell of a lot of *dinero* and Callicot was a greedy, little, fat bastard.

But Rimrock was going through a lot of agony now and he didn't care much about anything any more — not even the money.

"I'll go get you a doctor," Pinker said and he left.

But he didn't come back. And no doctor turned up. At least, Rimrock didn't think so. He was going through some kind of hot, agony-filled, delirious nightmare . . .

★ ★ ★

Having checked beforehand, Pinker knew where the halfway stop for the stage was and that it would stay there for a while to water the horses while the passengers slackened their stiff bones and then maybe had a drink and a bite to eat.

He rode across country and beat the stage to the place and he waited in the little station-cum-saloon-cum-eating place.

He had acted hastily. Sitting sipping rotgut rye, he admitted to himself now that he had kind of jumped the gun.

First off he should've slit Rimrock's throat and taken his bundle. Rimrock wasn't going to be any use to him any more. What did he owe Rimrock? Nothing! And he could pick up another partner any place should he need one.

161

Hell, he must be going soft. Or stupid.

Still, he had to go through with his other plan now. And, if he could find out from fat Lem Callicot who paid for that four-kill caper there could be rich pickings — and, also, he (Pinker) could make sure that nobody talked to anybody about anything any more.

The stage came in and he went out to meet it, strolling as if he had all the time in the world, wondering what sort of double-cross Callicot had in mind, a mite uncertain now but not showing it.

The shotgun-man got down from his perch beside the driver, bringing down with him a stool which he placed by the coach door for the folks to use as a step as they came down.

The driver sat disdainfully. He was the boss-man, didn't aim to get down till all the flim-flamming was finished, and his mate was welcome to the coins he might glean from anybody who had enjoyed the bone-shaking ride.

162

Lem Callicot was the second one down and he saw Pinker and his eyes shot wide in his little, fat, red face.

Pinker had left his horse nearby. He approached Callicot as the man, hesitating, puzzled, became detached from the others who were making for the ramshackle building to drink, eat, rest in a chair instead of on rocking slats.

The driver was getting down from his perch and the shotgun-man, his back to the two who now met, was talking to his mate. And Pinker said to Callicot, "Get your horse. We're going for a little ride. Things I wanted to ask you. Sort of unfinished business."

The young man had his thumb hooked in his belt very near to his gun.

Callicot said, "My side of it is finished. I told you. You've got your money. That's the end of it."

"Bear with me," said Pinker gently.

They rode away. The driver and his pard glanced after them but, inured to the peculiar ways of passengers, made no comment.

A little way out on the plain Pinker halted his mount and said, "Using your left paw, bucko, you can hand to me that little pistol you keep under your belt and hidden, by the tail o' that funny coat."

"It's awkward. I . . ."

"Try it." Pinker had his own gun out now, held it loosely. He smiled. "But don't try anything funny."

Gingerly, Callicot handed over his Bulldog pistol and Pinker tucked it into his own belt. He held on to his own gun. "Lead the way my friend," he said.

Presently he said, "This'll do."

It was a small grove of cottonwoods. All around it were the empty plains.

17

UNDER orders, Lem Callicot was dismounting when Pinker hit him a glancing blow on the head which pitched him to the grass, momentarily stunned.

When he was able to orient himself he looked up into the face of his attacker, and the two horses browsed nearby.

Pinker had sheathed his gun. His knife was in his hand. His eyes glittered strangely in the sunlight that came through the branches of the trees. Somehow his young face didn't seem handsome any more. He seemed to be labouring under some sort of bottled fury.

"What had you in mind, bucko?" he said. "What kind of tricks?"

"I don't know what you're talking about," said Callicot huskily. "Why . . . ?"

He broke off with a yelp as the sharp point of the knife drew a bloody line down his cheek.

"Next'll be your throat," Pinker said.

"I did my part," said the little, fat man. "All of it. You have no call to behave like this. What is the matter with you?" His voice was getting stronger. He was working himself up into a real state of indignation.

But he was as cunning as a coachload of monkeys. And Pinker said, "Oh, hell," and grinned without any mirth in his pitiless blue eyes and slashed downwards and cut him across the side of the neck.

"Oh, God," said Callicot and his voice died.

"Who set up those killings then?" demanded Pinker. "Who paid for 'em?"

"I don't know." The fat man's answer was little more than a whisper.

"You must know. I know how you operate. You'd have to . . . "

"Not always." The whisper was urgent

now. "I use a go-between. It was him . . . "

"Who was he?"

"I can't tell you. I don't . . . "

Callicot screamed then. As the knife flashed again and the blade sliced his throat and the blood ran faster.

"Who was he?" Pinker bent closer and the blade flashed before Callicot's eyes, the sun catching it, giving it a wicked fire. And then it was poised over the fat man's throat once more from which the blood flowed.

Callicot whispered again. The words were hardly audible. But Pinker caught the name, and maybe that was all he needed.

And then Callicot gave a huge sigh and seemed to collapse in upon himself, his eyes closing, an almost benign look on his plump features. He stopped whispering. He stopped breathing.

"Goddamit," said Pinker, straightening himself. "I cut him too deep."

But maybe it didn't matter any more if Callicot had given him the straights of it, that name. He (Pinker) had hardly been able to believe his ears. A name well known, even to him. And, then again, on thinking . . .

He bent and, absentmindedly, wiped the blade of his knife on Callicot's pants. He returned it to its sheath. He turned to the two horses.

He left the body where it was. The predators would find it. He took the spare horse with him, not forgetting to search the body before he left. He got another slice of *dinero*. Very acceptable. But nothing else of any great note.

* * *

After alighting from the train Jim Linlatter had to hire another trotting horse and a gig in order to get to his destination.

He was getting towards the Mexican quarters and he paused to ask directions from time to time. These were friendly, helpful people and he was an affable man. There were no difficulties. But what lay ahead?

He found the range. He saw the plentiful, fat cattle. He thought he saw the sun on the Rio Grande. But maybe that was only a mirage.

He saw no more people. But then he saw the gates: the entrance to the ranch-place proper.

An imposing crosspiece with burned upon it the inscription *Bar B Alverado.*

Sheriff Linlatter, who was not wearing his badge now, had learned that in these parts the ranch was known merely as the Bar B A. Staunch, straight gates wide open welcomingly. And Linlatter clicked his tongue and drove the little brown horse and the narrow high-seated gig through the gates and the wheels spun and sang on the hard-packed and well-swept dirt of the drive.

The drive wound like a regular trail and so far Linlatter only saw rooftop glimpses of the ranch buildings ahead.

There were fences each side of the drive. They were symmetrical and well kept. The grass each side was quite lush with very little bare brown as he had seen out on the plains. The sun beat down on him, but he had forgotten it. What lay ahead?

Something? What? This had the look of a proud and peaceful place. Had he, after all, with hopes or trepidation come all this way for nothing?

There were horses grazing but no beef now: that was out on the range and plenty of it and good.

The gig turned a bend in the drive and the ranch building stood ahead, bathed in an almost blinding sunshine. But black figures against that sun-blaze now. Black cut-out figures of men on horses hastening towards the visitor.

Linlatter counted five riders. But he couldn't see them clearly yet.

He did not see them clearly until they drew up in front of him. They all looked like Mexicans. But maybe that was because they all seemed to be wearing very wide-brimmed Mexican-style hats. But all kinds of folks wore those kind of hats down here, he remembered. Protection from the sun and the dust.

One man came forward, upright in the saddle, and he was indeed Mexican. A well-set up handsome young man who reminded Linlatter of his deputy Johnny back in Lobo Peaks.

The sun cut across them and they both squinted, the younger man with his head on one side. He was the first to speak. His English was good, but strangely formal.

"I think I know you," he said. "You are a Ranger and your name is Linlatter. James Linlatter."

"I'm Jim Linlatter. But I am no longer a Ranger. Maybe you will be pleased to hear that."

★ ★ ★

"We've got them," said wall-eyed Mack exultantly. "By Gar — we've got 'em."

"I don't see 'em," said Ed Gallion

sardonically. "So we ain't got 'em."

"Right," said tow-headed Jingo. "We've asked a lot of damn' questions and we've got a lot of answers, some of 'em matching up with what we've heard before. But none of that means a damn' thing if those folks have decided to change their minds."

"And that third man is a sort of unknown factor," said Johnny Tortuga. "Though you did say you might know who that is, didn't you, Cap'n Ed?"

"I'd opine who it might be that's all. A little fat snake called Lem Callicot. He could have set the whole thing up, those four killings. That's the kind of thing he does, but without gettin' any blood on his own fat paws o' course."

"There's nothing around here," said Jingo. "A whole lotta nothingness."

"There's a sort of new town someplace in this territory," said Mack. Then he added doubtfully, "Used to be."

"Towns come an' towns go," said

Jingo. "That'un, if it ever existed 'cept in your imagination, could be a ghost town now."

Mack didn't seem to have anything further to say on the subject until Gallion, seeming to come out of a quick think, asked him, "Was there a bank in this town?"

"I — I think so."

"A rail station?"

"No, I don't think so . . . but, wait a minute, I think a stage coach used to call there."

"Ghost banks," snorted Jingo. "Ghost stage coaches."

"Mebbe a ghost saloon also," said Johnny.

"Now you're talkin', pardner. As long as it has real hooch."

★ ★ ★

Back in Lobo Peaks, Jingo's ranchpards still felt as if they had sort of been cheated. Three of them did anyway and they were the three who had more time because they had done a lot of night line riding. And of course they decided to go into town again.

They had seen Sheriff Jim Linlatter call at the ranch to see their boss, and Linlatter's old friend Cy O'Day. The sheriff had been in a little gig and had still had his arm in a sling. One of the three rannies was the one who had hit the lawman but it was doubtful whether Linlatter had recognized which one it was in the mêlée.

They had watched the lawman leave the ranch and he hadn't been going back in the direction of town.

They learned later that the sheriff was off on his lonesome again to some place. Not that he would've been much problem with a busted fin, the three rannies told each other.

They didn't believe at first that that ancient goat called The Old Gunfighter was back in the territory again. And that (and this was the hardest part to believe) he had taken the place of the sheriff in the law office.

They aimed to find out what was what, however, and they set off for Lobo Peaks in high good spirits.

18

ALTHOUGH he wouldn't admit it to anybody, The Old Gunfighter was going deaf. At first he didn't hear the knocking on the door and the redheaded kid had to hammer really hard before, Navy Colt in hand, the oldster opened the door.

The kid gawked at the gun. The man holstered it, said, "Yeh, son?"

"There's a fight down in the saloon. Breakings. All sorts o' things . . . "

Now, vaguely, The Old Gunfighter could hear the noise.

"All right, I'll deal with it. Thank you. Go along now."

"Yes, suh."

Sid Mallow closed the door. Glasses or no glasses, his eyes weren't as good as they used to be either. The way he could still shoot, that must be due to some kind of instinct he thought. But he didn't want the rough work any more. Not if he could avoid it . . .

He picked up his second Navy Colt from off the desk. He had had the matching pair for quite a while now, but he had never been a twin-holster man.

He was a right-handed man. Although he could shoot quite well with his left hand — better than most he thought — he was better with the right. He had a holster on his right side and the one gun was back in there. He tucked the other one in his belt at the other side. He wouldn't have tried that with the big Dragoon — likely to shoot his privates off.

He was moving when, on an afterthought, he turned back a bit and picked up the shotgun which was sawn off at both ends, a stubby, wicked-looking, intimidating weapon.

He put on his battered slouch hat. That was an afterthought also. What in hell was the matter with him? Was he all at sixes and sevens?

He left the office, locking the door behind him. He straightened himself visibly as he went along the street.

A ragged old-timer was peering through the window of the saloon. He heard the bootheels and he turned and squinted. He saw Sid Mallow, The Old Gunfighter and he took to his heels. He went into an alley and, when Mallow pushed one hand against the batwing the other oldster was peering around the corner, watching and waiting to see what would happen next.

The noise was hitting the elderly gunslinger hard now. He hadn't noticed anybody else in the street, but a horse in the distance, maybe a man on it.

It was easy to see who were the cause of the disturbance. There were three of them and they were doing a jig in the centre of the floor, circling each other and whooping. Chairs lay upturned and there was the stink of spilled hooch to kill the odours of tobacco smoke and sweaty bodies. Some of the townies — regular barflies by the look

178

of 'em — were clapping their hands in time to the thundering bootheels. They didn't need any music, were making their own brand. Other folks stood about, sidled about, looking uncertain or sheepish.

The Old Gunfighter remembered that Jim Linlatter had told him that it was during such a saloon mêlée that he had gotten his arm busted. In this very saloon too.

It didn't seem that anybody had been really hurt yet, not by the look of it. But things were getting close to that way, fraught.

The townies looked at the newcomer. Most of them knew him. Some of them on the sidelines even greeted him, then sidled back out of harm's way.

"Look who's here," carolled one of the barflies.

The Old Gunfighter let loose one charge of the shotgun into the floor in front of the mob and folks scattered. There were reverberations and some dust and a sort of echo, which died.

And then all action was at end, was obviously suspended: one cowboy still had a leg in the air and he lowered it gently, silently, and nobody else moved at all.

The Old Gunfighter was pointing the twin barrels straight now and there was obviously another shell left in the gun.

As it would be, it was one of the cowboys who broke the silence.

"Look at the ol' man with his big shooter. Who does he think he is?"

"I don't need it," said The Old Gunfighter and he slung the shotgun behind him so that with a clatter it came to rest at the side of the batwings.

It didn't go off, could have peppered somebody or other; or more, even the old man himself. He didn't seem to care one way or the other.

The rannies had been drinking. They had blood in their eyes. Maybe the one who had spoken had imbibed more than the others, or he couldn't hold it so well, or he was just naturally reckless, or a consarned show-off.

He fell into a gunfighter's crouch and asked, with a growl, "What are you going to do now then, old man?"

Sid Mallow did not change his stance. He stood erect, very little stoop about his shoulders, his gnarled old hands hanging loosely at his sides.

"Don't try it, son," he said. "I would kill you."

One of the three boys was a bit older than the others, a longer stayer at the ranch, knew that The Old Gunfighter was well known to the boss. This boy — and he was no boy — was suddenly sober. "He would, Cal," he said. "He means it. He'd do it. He could."

The urgency in his pard's voice gave the would-be gunslinger pause for thought. He straightened up, his hands well away from his sides.

"Oh, hell," he said. "There ain't no fun here any more. Let's get going."

"Lay some *dinero* on the bar first,

boys," said the old man who stood between them and their means of exit. "You owe it."

The older ranny led the way, turning, pulling forth greenbacks, slapping them on the bartop. The one called Cal, in a last gesture, flung his across so that some of them spilled on to the floor at the other side.

The oldster by the doors stepped aside to let the three go by and he said, "I wouldn't come into town again for a while if I wuz you."

Disdainfully, they didn't look at him. They marched out. A little later hoofbeats signified that they were going away.

An old-timer blew out a loud breath and said, "Have a drink, Sid."

"I don't mind." The surrogate lawman collected his shotgun.

★ ★ ★

Rimrock didn't hear the rapping on his door. He lay in darkness and in his

182

delirium. He had been moaning and shouting.

The door opened slowly, groaning on its hinges. "What's the matter?" a plaintive female voice asked. "What's the matter?"

The noises came from the bed again, making no sense. A shaft of moonlight slanted across the tossing figure beneath the blankets.

"You're gonna lose them," she said. But she came no further into the room, stood with her tousled head stuck around the edge of the partially open door. Then, abruptly, she withdrew it. Her footsteps pattered in the passage, died.

They started up again. She came back carrying a lantern, its light throwing grotesque shadows on the walls, the wick smoking. Now she entered Rimrock's room and moved to the side of the bed.

Her sudden presence, and the yellow light, did something to the man in the bed. He stopped making his noises.

His whole life had been danger. His instinct for self-preservation was very finely honed, was an elementary *gut* thing. In his delirium he had lost it; but now it was awakened again.

He saw the girl in the light. He even recognized her, or thought he did. A local *puta*. Looked half-Indian. "You're a long way from home, ain't you, honey?" he asked.

"You look terrible, man," she said. "I'll go get the doc."

He didn't say anything any more. The spark had gone again. He had passed out completely.

He was roused, though, when the girl returned with a fat rumpled gent who smelled of booze and pipe-smoke. Rimrock became the little stoic, didn't yell when the man removed the sodden, blood-stained bandage.

"What happened to your face as well?" the doc wanted to know.

"That's an old thing," Rimrock croaked.

The fat man might have been boozing

a mite, but he was a deft professional. "God, this is a mess," he said. "It's going bad."

He bent to his bag, which was on the floor. He rose, grunting, and got to work. Some kind of salve which at first stung, making Rimrock curse involuntarily, but then chilled, soothed. And a draught of something to drink from a tiny, smoky glass.

"Rest," the doc said. "I'll see you in the morning."

Rimrock was already drifting off again and he was quiet. As the girl and the doctor went through the door the latter said, "I don't like that. I don't like that at all." Rimrock didn't hear him.

He woke during the night and he wasn't in so much pain. But he was scared and he didn't know what he was scared about. He had been wounded before and worse than this. But he had once known a feller who had died after being shot in the toe. Neglect!

But now he, Rimrock, was being

taken care of. He wondered where the little *puta* was at now. His thoughts drifted, however. . . Nah, he wasn't going to die. He reached for his gun. The feel of it was very comforting.

That gal, she could've cut his throat, could have robbed him. His hard-earned pay, the biggest haul he had ever had, was under the bed. He could've shot *her*, though . . .

He drifted. *Drifted* . . .

When he came-to again light was in the room. And so was Pinker. Grinning like a cat who had brought home a nice fat mouse.

But he had in fact killed a fat mouse and left it lying among the trees on the plains a long way away. He told Rimrock all about it and what he had learned and he was cocka-hoop. All of a smart gabble and still standing, looking down at the red-faced grotesquely-bandaged little man in the bed.

"You're a mess," he said at length. And then, as if he had had it on his mind all the time, "You ain't gonna be any use to me any more, or to yourself. I guess I better take your *dinero* and hightail."

He pulled his knife.

Using the gun he held under the bedclothes Rimrock let off two rapid shots through the blankets. Both slugs took Pinker full in the chest and slammed him backwards. The blade of his knife dug into the floor and quivered. Pinker's young face was suddenly grotesque and ugly. He skittered backwards on his bootheels and hit the door, which he had closed behind him when he entered the room.

His eyes stared. The eyes of an animal, poleaxed, dead. One of the bullets, not deflected by anything solid had gone right through his body, tearing a bigger hole in his back. He slid down the door, leaving red spider-trails on the worn, faded brown paint, and came to rest in a seated position, his head drooping then, face mercifully hidden.

Bootheels hammered in the passage outside. Rimrock drew his gun out on to the top of the bed. He wasn't focusing very well. He had tensed himself, knowing that Pinker was bound to pull something.

The fancy young bastard had killed Lem Callicot, after draining him. The fancy young bastard knew who had set up the four killings. And, this time, Callicot had been even more devious than usual and there had been a third party involved. Pinker had known who the hirer and payer was, and the third party. More pickings there he'd figured (working it out in his crazy brain) after Rimrock was eliminated.

Rimrock could hardly see the door but was aware that it had been opened forcibly, the body flung aside.

"Drop the gun, bucko," a voice said.

But he had already done that, couldn't hold it any longer. He muttered something. His head fell sideways and his eyes closed.

19

THREE men with shiny law badges. Cap'n Ed Gallion, ex-Texas Ranger; Johnny Tortuga, long-time deputy of Sheriff Linlatter of Lobo Peaks; and ranchhand-cum-deputy Jingo, also of Lobo Peaks territory.

And behind them lingering by the door a fourth man. He had no badge. He had a wall eye.

As if impelled by the collective gaze of the quartet, Rimrock opened his eyes again and looked from face to face. At first bemusedly, and then with a crazy sort of awareness, his eyes feverish and wild.

Then, suddenly, he began to laugh. But it was half a scream, a horrible sound.

Four men, a man in the bed, a sixth man, a body, which the four men skirted now. "God; can't we shut him up?" said the one called Jingo.

The others didn't say anything. And they all whirled in their tracks as the door was flung open behind them.

A girl came rushing in, screamed as she almost tripped over the body. But it did not stop her. She wore only a thin shift and the lines of her small but voluptuous body were well revealed, her breasts almost spilling from their concealment. Her eyes blazed in a swarthy, pretty face as she demanded, "What are you doing to that poor man?"

That Johnny Tortuga had a gun out didn't seem to faze her at all, even if she noticed the shining weapon. And she must have heard the gunshots.

A lot of other folk had heard the gunshots and now most of them seemed to be gathered in the passage outside, their enquiring voices ringing. Jingo, all law deputy now, went out to reassure them that officialdom had everything in hand, and he had the bearing and the badge to prove it.

Rimrock had quit his noise — and now everything seemed kind of quiet.

"It's all right, honey," said Rimrock gently. "I know these gents."

It was a half-truth. He didn't actually know all of them. But it sufficed. The girl became uncertain, even shy.

"Go along, honey."

"You sure? You sure you will be all right?"

"Yes, thank you, I'll be fine."

It was evident that he would never be fine again, that the poison was destroying him. But the girl went. She could do nothing else. And the man in the bed looked up at his visitors and said, "All right, gents. I've run my string. I'll tell you anything you want to know." He laughed and it was like a death rattle. "And 'cos of my friend an' what he told me, I know a lot more than I did before. It's a pity he tried to slit my gullet an' I had to shoot him. He purely loved talkin', did Pinker, and he was fancy with it. I ain't fancy, but I'll do my best."

He started to laugh again, started to cough. But he fought it, beat it. "All that *dinero* under the bed," he mocked. "And me on top of it. And all Pinker's swag an' he can't spend it in hell."

The fat doctor bustled into the room. "Me an' these gents are having an important discussion, Doc," Rimrock said. "Please leave us to get on with it."

The big grey-haired lawman looked at the medico and shook his head slowly from side to side, then jerked it. The doctor withdrew.

"All right," said Rimrock as if clearing the deck for a new hand. This was a game he was going to play to the finish.

★ ★ ★

The young Mexican ranchman's name was Esteban. He let the visitor, arm-in-sling, Jim Linlatter, rest up while the rest went on with their business, ranch business that couldn't be put off. Cattle to be sought, night riders to be trailed.

By the time the party got back, with a few cows but no miscreants, the visitor was fast asleep in a wide and soft feather bed.

It was easy for both of them, Mexican landowner and Anglo lawman to talk over the breakfast table in the morning with no interruption after the soft-moving servant girls had left them to their repast. And Esteban let his visitor set the story.

Four Texas Rangers who came after a Mexican *bandido* who had killed over the border; who came out of their jurisdiction and turned into a lynch mob determined to rid the world of somebody who had killed children and raped women. They caught the man and, although he screamed his innocence, they hung him on the spot.

The rest of his bunch — if there had been a bunch — had scattered. There were no witnesses. Only, later, a Ranger who bragged in his cups. A

Ranger with a conscience maybe.

"There was no real proof though. Nothing. But those four men left the service; had to I guess. One of them in particular was a friend of mine. His name was Rafe Renvane."

"I know."

"He never told me the real truth. And it's too late now."

"Nobody knows the real truth. About any of it."

"Those four men are dead. Executed you might say. But not by rope. Rafe Renvane was the last one, shotgunned to death on the main street of my town, Lobo Peaks."

"You were not part of it . . . "

"I wasn't."

"But you came here afterwards asking questions and my mother sent you away."

"She did. And I can't say I blamed her. The place was much smaller then."

"Yes. We have worked hard, and we have prospered. But my mother never forgot her son, my brother Carlos, who was executed by your people. She swore that some day she would take revenge."

"And she did."

"Yes, she did. I tried to talk her out of it, tried to tell her that it was all in the past. She screamed at me and called me filthy names, said I was a traitor to my family, had spit in the face of her and in the face of my dead brother. There was just the two of us, you see, and our father died many years ago and I barely remember him."

Linlatter listened as Esteban went on. Very few ranch noises came through the thick adobe walls. Just murmurs. A friendly bustle. The kitchen window was closed against the dust, but the kitchen was wide and the doors were open all along the passages and there were cool currents of air. This was a peaceful scene as the two men, the young and the not so young, talked of death.

"I was the youngest. Carlos was the first-born and my mother doted on him. Even when he went bad she would not see that; she closed her eyes to anything that might make him less in her eyes. And then that thing happened. I think myself that maybe Carlos wasn't responsible for the crimes for which, as you put it, he was executed. But, *Madre de Dios*, I knew that he and his friends were responsible for things just as bad. That was the way it was. He died and I mourned for him and then I put him behind me. But my mother did not do this. She never stopped mourning. And she waited. She was always the sort who would wait."

"But she had to set it up eventually, didn't she?"

"She was dying. She died exactly a week ago. But work goes on; life goes on."

They had spoken before briefly of the woman's demise. But now Linlatter said, "I heard that from folks before I got here. But she had set things up quite a while before that, hadn't she?"

"She was not too old. She was very surprised I think when she learned that she was to die from the malignancy of the insides. So she did not wait any longer. She called for a man, what would you say? — a go-between?"

"I guess," said Jim Linlatter. "I want to know what man."

* * *

Now I'm the talky one, Rimrock thought, I guess Pinker would've been proud of me. But Pinker had been taken away and only drying bloodstains on the floor denoted that he had ever been there.

And Rimrock was all through talking now. He was drained. He could only just see the four visitors now. They were not people. Yeh, well, he *knew* they were people. But now, to him, they were just tall, shimmering shapes that came and went — they could've been anything.

Maybe he was dreaming again.

Maybe something worse was happening and, maybe all along he had known it would happen. Did a man know . . . ?

Nah, not him, it couldn't be him, it couldn't happen to him. He remembered earlier times and there were no more shapes, everything was clearer. There were pictures in his mind.

He had been burned. He was just a tad. Strong. Could he have died then? Nah! Down in the Pecos country he had been knifed in the side and still bore the scar. That had been a feverish time. He had shot and killed the sodbuster who had done that to him.

That had been way back. Before he met Pinker. He might've known Pinker aimed to do him wrong at the end. But Pinker had saved him a couple of times. Pinker! Maybe they'd meet in hell. But not quite yet . . .

There had been that lawman in Prescott who had shot him in the back after him and Pinker had taken care of a fat cat somebody had wanted killed. The bullet had been spent, had gotten tangled in Rimrock's wool vest. the wound had healed in a week . . .

The ear! The ear was no longer there but sometimes felt as if it was. His head was burning. He was burning all over. And the pictures had faded.

"I want that doc," he croaked. "I want him back."

Jingo fetched the man. Little, fat, perspiring, bustling. Professional. Bending, breathing heavily, and exuding an odour of pipe smoke. Rimrock very still, eyes closed . . .

The doctor pulled the blanket up over the red, bandaged face, shutting out the sight which seemed even more grotesque now in the quietness and the stillness.

"I warned him," the little man said.

"He had run out his string," said Ed Gallion. "He was gonna hang anyway."

"He had guts," said tow-headed Jingo. "I'll give him that."

Had Rimrock heard that he would have liked it. It was a better epitaph than he deserved.

20

THERE hadn't been any rain for some time and the humidity was thick as stagnant soup. The slightest effort made a man sweat, his under-garments sticking to him like flies to poison-paper. Now there was sort of haze which partially veiled the brighter, early-morning sun, though the heat became more intense, the sun, like a ball of blood, appearing spasmodically through the veil.

Bodies didn't keep in these kind of conditions and, anyway, the undertaker said his improvised ice-house was beginning to resemble a bath-house or a root cellar with running water.

A quick funeral was arranged and the two dead gunfighters were buried in the same grave, though in separate coffins. It was said they had had a final falling-out and had shot each other to death. Nobody would know the rights of that — there had been no witness. But the story would grow, and one legend was good as another.

A local preacher uttered garbled incantations and there were a hell of a lot more sightseers at the graveside than there were mourners.

The three lawman visitors, with their wall-eyed companion, were there, as a matter of courtesy it seemed. They seemed impatient to get moving.

There was a little half-breed *puta* called Lellie who wept silently. Nobody knew whether she had anything to do with either, or both, of the two men. You never could tell with those frails. The local madam appeared and ushered Lellie away, together with others like her who were hanging around on the sidelines because they loved funerals. They hadn't actually been weeping, being all bleary-eyed anyway from being up earlier than usual.

The town was a buzz of early activity and the saloon did better than usual.

It was cool in there. The four visitors who had been in at the death, and the burial, did not hang around any more. Heat or no heat, they were on their way.

★ ★ ★

Esteban had said, "The other man was here too. The one they called 'the Cap'n'."

"I know," Jim Linlatter had said.

As he made his somewhat tortuous journey back home he wondered what was happening to Cap'n Ed Gallion, and to Johnny and Jingo.

He did not know that by then, Gallion, Tortuga, and Tortuga's friend and sparring partner Jingo, were no longer a trio, had become part of a quartet, having picked up a wall-eyed individual whom Sheriff Linlatter of Lobo Peaks had heard about but hadn't met.

Then things changed once more.

The killers, Rimrock and Pinker,

were dead. But there were others. And that was the reason the quartet split up, Johnny and Jingo to go on, and Gallion to go back, carrying the money.

Johnny and Jingo knew their approximate destination. If they didn't strike first off, they could go on from there. They were no respecters of persons, and they had tongues in their heads.

Gallion was going back fast. And wall-eyed Mack had said, "My cousin is dead. Ol' Josh. We'd been together for a long time. This thing ain't finished yet. I want to stay with you."

"All right," said Gallion.

They rode hard.

And, going in the other direction, Johnny and Jingo weren't doing so badly themselves.

Better, and more quickly; though, in the end, somewhat frustrating, a sort of anti-climax.

They were approaching a certain grove of trees that stood out on the empty plains when the three ragged old-timers came out of shelter and seemed to be literally bristling with guns.

Three men they thought, but one of them turned out to be a woman, wearing pants and a pair of hideously-scuffed leather *chaps* over them and a wideawake hat atop straggly greying hair with a small bun at the back. They only saw the bun later, for they were stopped dead. The woman held a levelled twelve-bore which made her companions' mundane pistols look like toys.

She was probably in her fifties and wore the weathered look of a real Western pioneer woman. The man who stood beside her was of about the same age, give or take a few years, but the third member of the party was older still, a bent and wizened old-timer who could be father to one of the other two.

Both Johnny and Jingo raised their paws in token peace signs. You couldn't argue with a battery of weapons like that lot and folks who looked as if they had been weaned on such armoury; not evil, but like trained workmen with much-used tools.

"Hallo, folks," said the grinning tow-head cowboy. "What goes down here now then?"

And his companion, the handsome Mexican boy with the pencil-thin moustache inclined his head as if he was greeting a fancy filly at a ball, and he smiled but said nothing.

"You been past this way before?" asked the younger of the two gun-toters.

"No, my friend," said Johnny Tortuga. "We are strangers here. We were riding peaceably till you stopped us."

"Can we put our hands down now?" asked Jingo. His grin was turning to a scowl.

But then his mouth fell open and he glanced sideways at his companion and said, "Will you look at that?"

She had come out of the trees, and she stood poised now. She was

young and she was slim. She wore a
slouch hat but in everything else she
was breathtakingly feminine, with long
reddish locks that cascaded over her
shoulders as if she had just shaken
them free from confinement, giving
her a sort of abandoned look, though
her stance was demure.

The younger of the two men who
stood beside the gun-toting woman,
half-turned his head, said, "Dru, I
asked you to stay in there." There
was no harshness in his voice like
the harshness he had used on the two
strangers.

"I'm all right, Pa, I'll come to no
harm."

"They're lawmen," the older woman
said.

"That don't mean nothin' nowadays,"
said the wizened old-timer.

"You can lower your hands," the
other man said. "But we're gonna keep
our guns on you."

"That's your privilege, *amigo*," said
the Mexican deputy.

The other man went on. "There's a body back in the trees. The vultures have been at it. We covered it with a blanket. We don't know who the man was, but it looks like he could've been some kind of dude. A little jasper but plenty of flesh on him."

"Not as much as there was afore them pesky birds got at him," said the wizened old-timer with a nasty cackle.

"Stow it, Pa," said the older woman.

"Can we light down?" said Jingo.

The guns bristled. "Easy," said the woman. "Easy." She might be partly reassured by the looks of the silver badges the two newcomers wore on their breasts, but she wasn't taking any chances.

She had been handsome and the likeness to her lovely daughter was still in her face, but she held a shotgun like she might have held a long-handled kitchen broom, with a look of expertise and industry. And it took no effort to pull a trigger, or two at once beneath the formidable hammers.

Jingo and Johnny moved like cats and kept their hands well away from their own weapons.

The girl went ahead of them. She was slim-waisted, trim, with a fascinating wiggle. Her name, they knew, was Dru, short no doubt for Drusilla.

The old-timer kept over to the side of her. The man and wife kept behind the two deputies. All three kept their weapons at ready.

"Stay outa this, Dru," the father told the girl.

She needed no command, stayed just inside the edge of the trees as far away from the centre of the small clearing as possible. And nobody could blame her. The stench was noticeable now and far from pleasant.

The rest of the company surrounded the blanket-covered form which lay in the grass. Johnny Tortuga stooped and moved the blanket to one side, his handsome features wrinkling in disgust as he did so. And then the sight that was revealed intensified the unpleasantness. There was no need to stay down long though. Johnny whipped the covering back over the corpse and he said, "It's a mess. But it's the man called Callicot, no doubt, I would think. Even the way he is now he answers to the description Rimrock gave us and Ed Gallion added to, remembering Callicot from the old days, though the Cap'n said the man was probably less fat then."

"He was fat all right," cackled the old-timer. "A tasty morsel all right."

"For Godsakes, Pa," said the woman.

"It was him all right," said Jingo. "An' he's bin almost stripped and them birds did the rest."

"We'd best bury him," said Johnny.

"What's that?" said Jingo, and he was pointing.

It was the other side of the trees, parts of it revealed through gaps between trunks and branches. "It looks like a covered wagon," Jingo added.

"It is a covered wagon," said the older woman scornfully. "It belongs to us, for Pete's sake."

"We've got some shovels," the old-timer said. "I'll go get 'em."

When the task was done, Johnny and Jingo returned with the four folks and their wagon to the town they hadn't left long ago and to where the family had been heading. They didn't learn the names of the delectable Dru's parents or her grandpa and were not much interested in this information.

Then again, to get to know the family would undoubtedly have helped them to get to know Dru better and to both of them that would have been a prime accomplishment, although it could have led them to becoming sparring partners again.

As it was, though, they had to be on their way again, and *pronto*. They had friends who would probably need their help. They had learned that from their wagon, tall and in a colourful orange-coloured canvas, the family sold medicines, elixirs and suchlike, which the cackling grandpa made himself, was noted for such things. The townsfolk came out to greet the wagon and some of them already had their wants jotted down on scraps of paper or had bottles they needed refilling.

But the two disgustingly healthy law deputies were not in need of such vapories and rode carefully through the growing press and then out of town and onwards.

Again they rode pretty hard.

They carried with them an image of a pretty, red-haired girl, hoped she wouldn't pass from their ken forever, that sometime the tall orange-canvased wagon would pass their way once more.

"I told her where we wuz at," shouted Jingo over the thunder of the hooves.

Johnny gave him a sardonic sidelong glance.

21

THE back door of the jail was locked but Sheriff Linlatter had a key on the ring attached to the side of his belt.

He had always kept the hinges well oiled. The door opened silently. Then he was in the passage which ran alongside the cells, both of which were empty.

The other door was closed but he figured that with no prisoners it wouldn't be locked. He was right. Soon he was in the office and The Old Gunfighter, seated at the desk, turned his head towards him.

By this time Jim Linlatter had his grubby arm-sling dangling and his gun out. He pointed it at the older man and said, "Now tell me why. Tell me all about it."

Sid Mallow said, "At first I didn't

wonder about your trip. Then I started to do some figuring. You've been down on the border, ain't you?"

"I have. Stand away from the desk."

Mallow did as he was told. He seemed to be unarmed.

Linlatter said, "I'm gonna lock you in a cell. An' then we'll talk. I see you have the keys there. Pick'em up."

"You don't have to do this, Jim."

"Don't I? I'm doin' it anyway. Pick up them keys like I said."

"We can talk here. I've got a lot to tell you."

"I'll bet. Do as I say, or by Gar I'll slug you." Linlatter began to move forward.

Mallow picked up the heavy ring with its bunch of keys from the desk and, in the same effortless motion, swung them in an arc at the end of his long arm. They caught the sheriff on the temple, staggering him. His gun went off but, by then, it was pointed at the roof and brought down a shower of plaster.

Mallow hit out again with the keys, slashing Linlatter's wrist, so that he gave an involuntary shout of pain and dropped the gun.

With a heavy boot Mallow kicked him in the kneecap.

Linlatter's leg gave way beneath him. As he slumped maybe he could have reached the gun then. But Mallow beat him to it, scooped it up, stepped back and leaned against the desk and pointed the Colt at the disabled sheriff who, grunting, was trying to haul himself upright again.

Mallow reached behind him and raked his own gunbelt from the other side of the desk. In a swift movement, he whipped the belt around his waist and shoved the spare gun in the front of it as he drew his own weapon, obviously feeling more comfortable with it.

For an infinitesimal moment the sheriff could have had a slight edge, but he hadn't been in a position to take it. Now he finally straightened up. He was unsteady though, and obviously in pain with his bruised knee, his arm, and the whack on his head which made his eyes look glazed, and still surprised. He had had too many surprises lately. He was bemused by them and the treatment he had received because of them.

But his erstwhile friend of long standing, The Old Gunfighter, didn't look any different than he had ever looked except for the menacing gun.

The Old Gunfighter said, "Turn around, Jim. You're the one who's going in a cell."

★ ★ ★

He left Linlatter in the cell, wouldn't talk to him, left him, his grimy sling around his neck, nursing his bruised knee with one hand and looking lost.

He made sure that the sheriff was locked in the cell. It was quiet out there after Linlatter had quit asking querulous questions, had gotten no answers. Back in the office Mallow made sure the front door was locked. He had already ascertained that the back door was. Linlatter must have done that after he came through. For a man with a damaged arm he hadn't done so badly. He was more damaged now. He would keep.

Mallow had all his gear back in his tarp and was about to tie it together when the door was rapped. He hadn't heard any hoofbeats, any footsteps even. He went over to the window. By moving the curtain gently aside and craning his neck he could see on to the sidewalk. He had done a bit of spying like this before and knew that if callers were not too near to the door he would be able to see them. He adjusted his spectacles more securely on his eagle nose.

This caller was Doc Beedle and he was standing back on the sidewalk. He glanced at the window and Mallow drew back quickly, hoped he hadn't been spotted. Another old friend. They

216

were coming out of the woodwork, goddamit!

The tall doctor rapped the door again. Mallow catfooted over to the desk. Then he changed his mind and retraced his steps and stood against the wall between the door and the window. It was a good move, and only just in time. There were movements outside the window, scratchings against the glass. Beedle was obviously peering through the window. Mallow didn't know whether this old friend could see the interior well, but he was having a damn' good try at seeing something or other.

He seemed to move. The voice came from the other side of the door.

"Jim! You in there, Jim?"

Mallow was startled. Beedle must have seen Jim Linlatter come back into town. Had they talked?

"Jim. Can you hear me, Jim?"

No reply. And Mallow waiting, wondering what to do next. Could Linlatter back in the cell hear that

217

voice? Mallow didn't think so, or Jim would have answered. Unless he had passed out.

The voice sounded again. "Sid. Sid Mallow. Are you in there?"

The latch was rattled. Why hadn't he tried that before? Was he wary? Did he know more than he should? Hell, no, even Jim Linlatter didn't know the all of it. How could the doc . . . ? Footsteps: he heard them now, though the tall medico was soft-moving, a gentle cuss under all his bluster.

And now dead silence.

The doc's voice hadn't been over-loud. It never was unless he was shouting at an obstreperous patient who wouldn't take heed and do what was best for him. There was no more from out back, though Sid Mallow listened intently now. He realized that, the way it was built, the jail section of the four-square building was pretty soundproof. At the desk, he went back to what he had been doing when the interruption had occurred.

* * *

With a puzzled look on his long face, Doc Beedle was walking down the main street when he saw the two riders coming towards him. The badge-toting, moustached Ed Gallion and a wall-eyed gink who looked familiar but not too much. And Gallion was a reliable gent. The doc hastened to meet them.

"Somep'n up, Doc?" asked Gallion. He seemed edgy.

"Well, I dunno. A little while ago I saw Jim Linlatter come in. I wanted to talk to him, see how his arm was, the idiot. But I didn't have a chance. That pesky Mrs Boult, who is always turning up with some imaginary ailment, waylaid me. But as soon as I got rid of her I went down to the office. The door's locked. I called out but I didn't get any reply . . . !"

"How about The Old Gunfighter?" said Gallion sharply. "We called in at the ranch, saw Cy, learned the old man was here."

"No reply I said. If The Old Gunfighter is in the law office he wasn't letting on."

"Have you seen him around town?"

"No. Is something going on?" Beedle was an astute old bird.

"Things ain't exactly the way they used to be," said Gallion. "You go back to your surgery, Doc. We'll call you if we need you."

That last sentence had an ominous ring and the tall healer reacted to it. "If you might need my help I want to be . . ."

Gallion cut him short with scant courtesy. "Do as I say. I haven't got time to argue with you."

"All right," said Beedle huffily and he swung on his heels; marched.

"He's got sense," said Gallion, looking at his companion, the wall-eyed gunfighter known as Mack. "You

220

want to have some and step back outa this now, my friend?"

"I don't think I have that kinda sense, Mr Gallion," said Mack softly.

"So be it then. Come on."

roused to issue forth, go there, back outs this now, my friend."

"It's . . . this . . . thing . . . it . . . what is it?" All . . . Thurio said, "We should stop, it must . . . come on.

22

H E heard the sound of hooves, heard the clatter as the horses were halted, hitched maybe at the rack outside, or just left, reins dangling. He didn't go over to the window. He heard the bootheels on the boardwalk, then the door was tried. It was a stout door and it was locked. It didn't budge.

The door was rapped. He remained still, silent, leaning on the desk, watching the door. Bootheels scuffed. The door was rapped again.

A voice called, "You in there, Jim? Open the door."

There seemed to be a soft altercation out there. How many men? Sid Mallow wondered. Who? The posse? But what did the posse know anyway? Would the posse be after him?

"You in there, Mallow?" the voice

222

asked from outside, no anger there yet.

The next thing will be the back door, The Old Gunfighter thought. He would have to do something. Before *they* did something . . .

"You better answer," the voice said.

Ed Gallion, thought The Old Gunfighter: he was sure now. But who was with Gallion?

He left the desk, went back into the cell-block, the bunch of keys in one hand, his gun in the other. Linlatter was sitting on the bunk, his sling still looped around his neck, his damaged arm resting across his lap.

The Old Gunfighter had left the communicating door open and the door outside was being knocked harder now and Linlatter heard the noise.

"What's going on?" he asked. "You're in kind of a bind now, uh, Sid?"

Mallow unlocked the cell door. "Come on," he said, gesturing with the gun.

"You're letting me out, huh, and

coming out to join my friends?"

The other man had no answer to that. He backed, gestured again with the gun. Linlatter walked out of the cell and went ahead of him and through the door into the office.

"Stop in the middle there. Keep away from the desk."

At the command, Linlatter halted. There were scuffling sounds from outside. Were they moving? But then the door was hammered and Gallion's voice shouted, "Open up!"

Mallow moved up behind Linlatter. The older man had handcuffs clinking now in one hand in the place of the keys which he had put on the desk.

"Put both your hands behind your back."

"I can't. Not with this one arm like it is now. That just ain't possible."

"Put your good hand round here then."

"All right," said Jim Linlatter, almost affably.

Mallow put one cuff on and pulled.

"Get down on your knees."

"Hey, wait a minute!" No hint of affability now.

"Do as I say or I'll slug you. Don't waste my time." Mallow yanked with the free cuff and Linlatter was forced down and Mallow fastened the free cuff to one stubby leg of the heavy desk.

"Put that other arm back in the sling and stay like that an' don't try anything."

Outside the voice said, "If we don't get any answer we're coming in."

"They know," said Linlatter. "I don't know how they know, but they certainly know something."

"Shut up!" Then Mallow raised his voice. "Jim Linlatter is in here an' if anything is done to that door he's gonna get shot. You hear me?"

"We hear you."

"Whatever they know, you've burned your boats now anyway," said Linlatter. "But why, Sid? Why all of it?"

"Reasons," said The Old Gunfighter scornfully. "Sometimes you've got reasons and sometimes you ain't . . . !"

"Rafe Renvane was killed because of you. He was your friend for Godsakes."

"I know." And suddenly it was as if Sid Mallow wanted to justify himself, if that was possible. There was something in his voice . . . "You saw Esteban I guess."

"I did."

"I'm a roamer, you know that. I allus have been. I know those borderlands as much as I know the territory round here. More so maybe . . . "

There was an urgency in his voice now as he went on (and outside there didn't seem to be any noise, as if the folk out there were trying to figure what to do). "Esteban's father was a friend of mine. He died young. I still kept in touch with the family. Then Esteban's brother was killed. But I guess you know all about that . . . "

"Not all maybe. Enough."

"It did bad things to his ma. She swore that those who were responsible. would pay. But she had that fatalistic

Mexican patience and she waited. And the ranch that her husband had started was doing well. Esteban is clever and industrious. Maybe they were better off without the other boy, though of course his ma could never have seen that . . . "

"Cut it short, man. She became sick."

"Yes. And she enlisted my aid. She had a list. Names in a sealed envelope. I gave the sealed envelope to that sneaky, little fat go-between, Callicot."

"Hell, you were the go-between!"

"In a sense, yes. And I knew that Callicot was gonna use Pinker an' Rimrock. But I didn't know what names were in the envelope. I didn't know Rafe Renvane's name was in there. Not till I came back here . . . "

"Why did you stay? Why did you take this job as well?"

"I dunno. Maybe I thought I could make amends in some way . . . "

"Horse-shit!"

"I thought I might get a line on Pinker and Rimrock, deal with them. And Callicot again."

"Double bull-shit," said Linlatter.

But Mallow wasn't listening to him any more. "They're coming round the back," he said and he loped over to the communicating door which he had left ajar after he and his captive came through it.

Jim Linlatter heard him shout, "Back off. Or I'll kill the sheriff." His voice was hoarse, and almost querulous. Suddenly it had sounded like an old man's voice. An old man at the end of his tether.

If there was any reply from outside Linlatter couldn't hear it. All he heard then was the scuff of The Old Gunfighter's bootheels as he came back along the passage. Then he came through the door, and he said, "I hate being penned. We're going through that front door and you'll be my hostage."

"I ain't going any place with you again, old man," said Jim Linlatter.

"You are. Get up." Sid Mallow pointed the gun straight at his old friend.

The sheriff began to struggle to his feet. He was awkward, hampered by the handcuffs, his bad arm, his bruised knee. He slipped and came down hard on the floor and he yelled.

"Goddamit," said Mallow, bending forward. Linlatter was half on his back, half-sitting against the desk, half-lying really; looked as uncomfortable as a wounded upside-down bug. But he had the energy to swing his legs, his feet, shod as they were in heavy riding boots.

One boot caught Mallow hard and painfully on the shin and he staggered back, hissing with pain. Linlatter lashed out with his feet again and, groaning, missed. The older man righted himself and swung outwards and downwards with the heavy Colt.

The barrel of the gun struck Linlatter solidly on the side of the head and he slumped back against the desk, his eyes rolling, then closing altogether.

Sid Mallow left him, went over to the door, turned the key which he had left in the lock. He flung the door open with his free hand and crouched low as he went through with the gun pointing out in front of him.

Mack, who had been left on watch while Gallion went round back, was taken completely by surprise. The tall old man in the steel-rimmed spectacles cannoned into him, sending him spinning. He caught his heel on the edge of the boardwalk and spun, falling, striking his head on the bar of the hitching rack where the horses stood and were alarmed now, jerking and prancing. The man momentarily blacked out.

Sid Mallow ran on down the street. His horse was at the livery stable. He could've grabbed one of those from the rack. He hadn't thought. He was cursing under his breath as he ran awkwardly on his high-heeled riding boots. He hoped that character he had felled would stay down. He had a way to go.

Mack was up and his rifle was within reach in its saddle boot on his horse next to him. "Keep still, you jackass," he said and he managed to get the Winchester loose, raised it.

Ed Gallion came running out of the alley beside the jail and right into Mack's line of fire.

"Get down," screamed the wall-eyed man with the ridiculous wispy beard. He looked mad as a hen in a mudhole.

With a startled glance over his shoulder, Gallion dropped to one knee, looked after the running Sid Mallow, raised his own handgun.

Mack's shot almost took Gallion's hat off and there was an element of farce about things now, though neither of the men could possibly have recognized that.

And Sid Mallow, The Old Gunfighter, had disappeared into the livery stables.

He reappeared almost immediately, astride his horse. He had no saddle, just a blanket. He clung to the beast's flanks with his knees and urged him to a gallop.

Suddenly there was somebody else between him and the two men who were after his hide: Doc Beedle, striding, moving fast.

Ed Gallion waved his arms, shouted at the doc, but the doc didn't get out of the way fast enough. The horse and rider were a diminishing cloud of dust — and there were other folk down that way now. It was as if Injun smoke signals had been spotted and folks were appearing to take a look. And the shot. The rifle-twang, the echoes of which had died away. And the hoofbeats of The Old Gunfighter's horse had faded too.

Gallion gestured in the direction of the office. "Jim's in there, Doc. He might be hurt."

"But what . . . ?"

However, the two men were on their horses, then riding, the tall medico choking on their dust. Coughing, he went through the open door of the law office.

Sheriff Linlatter was scrambling to his feet. "Hallo, Doc," he said, smiling weakly.

23

SID MALLOW reached the draw; the rocks around it. He was all through running. He felt kind of naked. He had no saddle and he was bone-shaken. And this was no newly-broken maverick, this was a horse that was used to a saddle, all the accoutrements, a horse that seemed a mite disgruntled now. Mallow dismounted from him, left him ground-hitched by some sweet grass.

This was as good a place as any to light down in, the man thought. Better than most. Good for defence. Appropriate. He had spent a lot of time here over the years. At intervals. With his weapons. Practising. Why had he taken the trouble? Maybe just for the hell of it as the saying was.

He had weapons now, but not so many as he could have had. He had left the tarp which contained much of the stuff back in the law office. There might have been a bigger posse outside that place than he had figured and he had needed his hands free. Hell, they could've filled him full of holes.

As far as he knew now there had only been Ed Gallion and his ugly companion, though they could've gotten reinforcements by now of course — that was likely.

Whether or not, he would wait here. He had done some quick figuring. The line hut on the north range which he had been allowed to use by his old friend, rancher Cy O'Day wouldn't give much cover and protection. He hadn't left anything important there anyway, nothing like the stuff he had left back in the law office.

There he had left back-up gear. The odd guns, and 'odd' indeed some of them certainly were. Valuable, though. The Smith and Wesson silver-chased .44 calibre belly gun. And, also a .44, but a much bigger gun all told, the long-barrelled, powerful Colt Dragoon. And the cut-down derringer-like pistol of indeterminate gender which held more shots than any derringer could.

The Winchester repeater of course. And the sawn-off shotgun with the cut-down butt, plus the huge Bowie knife . . .

Still and all, here now he had his matching Navy Colts and the Peacemaker he had taken from Jim Linlatter. Pity he had had to slug Jim. Still, that had been better than shooting his head off. He hoped Jim was gonna be all right.

He had an extra gun here too; yes, he had. He went to collect it from where it was hidden under a pile of small polished rocks.

It was his oldest weapon. He had had it much longer than any of the others, even the Navy Colts. He had felt it to be too heavy to tote to Lobo Peaks with him and he hadn't figured he'd need it there. A Henry rifle.

Most folks would prefer the more

up-to-date Winchester model, he knew, but he felt more comfortable with the old Henry. He liked its weight, as he liked the weight of the Dragoon handgun, and was faster with both of them, he thought, than with anything else, though he toted the two Navy Colts most times for lighter weight. He was a strong old dog and not too good at new tricks.

He discovered that he didn't have a whole lot of cartridges for the Henry, and that was a pity. But he had plenty for the Navy Colts and some for the Peacemaker. He got himself a good well-covered vantage point and he put his guns around him, the Henry nearest to his hands.

He waited. They would have to come through the draw, but he would be able to see them long before that. His hearing wasn't what it used to be, but his eyes in their spectacles were pretty good.

He saw them before he heard them. And there were only two of them.

He raised the Henry to his shoulder. He waited till they were in range and then he squeezed the trigger three times as rapidly as possible, knowing even so that he was hitting where he aimed. He was *that* good with the reliable, beautifully-cared-for, old, long gun!

★ ★ ★

The bullets, spaced, hit in front of the two horses, making them rear. The echoes of the shots rolled away into the distance and died. But the noise didn't. The horses' hooves came down hard on the sunburned brown grass and the hardness beneath, and the two riders fought with the reins and cursed.

"Move apart," yelled Ed Gallion.

"God, that was some shooting," said Mack. "What . . . ?" His words broke into a yell as he was almost tossed from the saddle.

Gallion was managing to gentle his steed. He said, "The Old Gunfighter has an old Henry and he's mighty good with it. He could've killed us both. He's playing with us."

"Keep still, you damn' jackass." Mack was talking to the horse.

The beast was taking heed now.

"Get down," said Gallion. "We've got no cover here at all."

They both scrambled out of the saddle, tried to keep the horses between themselves and the draw, the rocks.

"Run him," Gallion yelled, pointing past Mack.

The latter got the older man's drift, held on to the reins, ran with the horse.

Gallion did the same, going off in the other direction. He wondered whether Mack felt as big a fool as he did.

Neither of them were going straight at all, but they were getting gradually near to the mouth of the draw and the horses, poor beasts, were spasmodic cover — if Sid Mallow didn't start shooting at moving human legs under horseflesh bellies.

But Sid had another ploy. He started to put shots behind the horses and they started to gallop and the men had difficulty in holding on to the reins. They ran. They were dragged. The Old Gunfighter rested the long gun.

Look at 'em go!

But he had to stop them before they reached the rocks and cover. So maybe his ploy hadn't been such a smart one after all! The two men were literally being dragged more quickly nearer to the rocks.

He could shoot the horses. But horses had always been good to him, better than many humans had. You could trust a good horse.

He could disable the men . . .

He raised the rifle again. Slowly . . .

24

"I HEARD somep'n," said Jingo. "In the far distance. But it sounded like shooting."

"I didn't hear anything," said Johnny Tortuga. "Mebbe it was a trick of the wind."

"There ain't much wind. Hold up, *amigo*." The big tow-headed boy reined in his horse.

The Mexican deputy with the handsome features and thin moustache followed his friend's example. Now they could hear the faint soughing of the wind but nothing more than that, no tricky sounds. The grasslands stretched ahead of them to infinity, nothing to break their brown and green monotony.

"We're yet too far from town to hear anything from there," said Johnny.

"No, we ain't in sight of the rocks and the draw yet. It's hazy out there."

241

"I'm sick already o' squinting an' listening. Come on."

"Just as you say, pardner." Jingo urged his horse on. Johnny and his mount kept pace with them.

Johnny was the first to speak after they had been riding in silence for a while, not pushing themselves or the horses.

"By Gar, I heard somep'n then."

"Me too," ejaculated his big *compadre*. "And it is shooting. Snapping. Echoing. Sounds like rifle-fire."

They both reined in again. And then they couldn't hear anything any more. It was exasperating.

Johnny shaded his eyes and peered into the distance. "I can see the rocks. If there was shooting I guess that's where it came from."

"We weren't imagining things this time," affirmed Jingo. "And we weren't last time if it comes to that. The breezes are blowin' this direction and the sound carried to us even back there."

"Agreed," said Johnny. "Well, let's go on then. We're supposed to be law deputies, ain't we?"

"C'mon then. But watch yourself. Keep apart."

"I know what I'm doing," said Johnny caustically.

★ ★ ★

He had put bullets all around them as they bounced on the ground. He hadn't hit either of them. And he certainly hadn't hit a horse. The two beasts were still galloping, really had their bits between their teeth. And he could see their wild eyes now.

These boys are getting bruised, he thought, and I could've nicked one or the other of 'em; I certainly threw stuff in their faces.

I can't disable them, he thought. Damn it, I can't!

Both men were separated from their horses now and were running, the horses going with them, the men full into the rifleman's gaze and then out again. Horses . . . Men . . . Horses hiding men. The rifleman put the old Henry down on the rocks.

Ed Gallion was scrambling into shelter. His companion wasn't far behind him in that, though there was still a sizeable gap between them.

If they used their heads they could flank me, thought the third man, in the rocks. Then what would they do? And what would he do? He was a free spirit, always had been. He would sooner die than spend the rest of his years incarcerated.

He had to get out of there!

He had to be quick. Before those two jaspers got nearer to him, spotted his position. He took another look out. He couldn't see either of the men now. And the horses, their wild run finished, were browsing on the grass just outside the perimeter of the rock outcrops on the edge of the draw.

He had picked himself a sort of nest in the rocks and now he had to climb to get out of it. It was not a hard climb, not much of an actual climb at all, more like going carefully from stepping stone to stepping stone, though there was no stream

He held the heavy long gun away from him and stepped carefully on his high-heeled riding boots, balancing himself, stepping from one rounded boulder to another. As quickly as possible so that his back wouldn't be shown to his pursuers should they begin to move quickly now.

The rocks were smooth and hard and bone-clean from the sun. The man slipped on one of his heels in the boots that were not made for walking. His arms flailed as he strove to keep his balance. He lurched, his long torso tilting backwards.

The heavy gun was jerked from his grasp and fell. As he involuntarily turned his head towards it, it went off.

There was no more shooting. And Gallion and Mack came together and crouched down and waited. If nothing else, they needed the rest.

The older man was bruised about the face and one of his elbows was skinned. His companion had a nose-bleed which he managed to stanch now with a grimy kerchief. They both looked as if they had been dragged by an irate bullock through a patch of prickly pear.

"Neither of us have fired a goddam shot yet," Mack said.

"We haven't had a chance, have we? And that old man could have killed us both five times over. I'm gonna give him a call."

Gallion raised his voice, shouted, "You there, Sid?"

There was no reply.

"What're you doin', you ol' goat?"

The breeze among the rocks answered mockingly after the small echoes had died.

"He's lit out," said Mack.

"We didn't hear any horse."

"He'll lead him. I guess he ain't mounted yet."

"That last shot," said Gallion musingly. "It didn't come our way. It didn't seem to go anyplace."

"That's right."

"Let's move."

They were not menaced. There was nothing to menace them any more.

They saw the Henry rifle first, shining in the sun. Its muzzle was blackened, the steel torn near the sight.

"He dropped it I guess," said Gallion softly. "That was the single shot we heard. It let itself off on the rocks."

The Old Gunfighter was hidden from them. They had to climb over rocks to find him. He had fallen into a dip. He lay on his back. His spectacles had fallen off but lay unbroken beside him. His eyes were open, staring up at the sun. He didn't look as if he was in pain, just surprised. There was a hole in the front of his head, at the sparse hairline.

"Shot by his own gun," said Mack in awe.

"I guess that's kind of appropriate,"

said Ed Gallion softly.

He sat down heavily on a boulder. Both he and Mack had miraculously held on to their hats. Gallion took his off and reached out and was about to place it over the dead face when he changed his mind. He replaced it on his head.

He rummaged inside his vest and came up with a red and white spotted bandanna that was far cleaner than the one Mack had produced a little earlier.

Ed Gallion covered The Old Gunfighter's face with great care. Mack was still on his feet. "Listen," he said. "I'm sure I heard hoofbeats."

"I heard 'em," said Gallion. "Let's take a look."

They made their way to the edge of the draw. They saw the two approaching riders and recognized them. Gallion waved his arms and shouted.

★ ★ ★

The funeral was a good one. Many of the townsfolk of Lobo Peaks weren't quite sure what had happened to The Old Gunfighter. But they had liked him. They turned up in force and celebrated his demise in the way that Western townships peculiarly did when they lost one of their own.

They had heard that The Old Gunfighter had had a sort of falling out with his old friend, Sheriff Linlatter; but the big moustached man was there large as life at the graveside. His face was a mite bruised and he still had his arm in a sling, had taken it from around his neck after Doc Beedle spoke sharply to him.

When the populace moved down Boot Hill to the main street a tall covered wagon was coming along. It was orange-covered and colourful. It was seen that deputies Johnny and Jingo went ahead hastily to meet it.

Some folks thought there might be shenanigans or something — till they saw the red-haired girl. And she seemed to know the two deputies right well.

Almost a day passed before the red-headed boy called Lenny knocked hastily on the law office door and, when Jim Linlatter opened it, said, "You better come down to the saloon, Sheriff. Johnny and Jingo are fightin' again."

THE END

ATCHISON LIBRARY
401 KANSAS
ATCHISON, KS 66002